"I don't know who you are."

Her face crumpled and she looked ready to pitch forward.

He had to do better than that. He dragged his hands out of his pockets and held them out in supplication.

"I have some memory, but some things... I know you—" he clenched his fist and pounded it against his chest "—here, but I don't know who you are. I don't know your name."

Silent tears dripped from her eyes. Wiping her hand across her nose, she drew in a shuddering breath. "I'm Devon. Devon Reese. I'm your... We were engaged."

Kieran squeezed his good eye closed and whispered her name. "Devon. Devon."

Yes, the name filled him with warmth and longing, those feelings belonging to his hazy past. They *had been* engaged. A woman like Devon, filled with golden light and promise, would never want a damaged man like him.

CAROL ERICSON

EYEWITNESS

Harlequin®

TORONTO NEW YORK LONDON
AMSTERDAM PARIS SYDNEY HAMBURG
STOCKHOLM ATHENS TOKYO MILAN MADRID
PRAGUE WARSAW BUDAPEST AUCKLAND

To the detectives of the TRAP West team for all their little bits of information regarding police procedures and protocol.

Recycling programs
for this product may
not exist in your area.

ISBN-13: 978-0-373-74676-7

EYEWITNESS

Copyright © 2012 by Carol Ericson

www.Harlequin.com

Printed in U.S.A.

ABOUT THE AUTHOR

Carol Ericson lives with her husband and two sons in Southern California, home of state-of-the-art cosmetic surgery, wild freeway chases, palm trees bending in the Santa Ana winds and a million amazing stories. These stories, along with hordes of virile men and feisty women, clamor for release from Carol's head. It makes for some interesting headaches until she sets them free to fulfill their destinies and her readers' fantasies. To find out more about Carol, her books and her strange headaches, please visit her website, www.carolericson.com, "where romance flirts with danger."

Books by Carol Ericson

CAST OF CHARACTERS

Kieran Roarke—A former prisoner of war, damaged and alone, he's compelled to return to Coral Cove and the woman who got him through his imprisonment, even if he can't remember her name. Once he meets her, and the son he hadn't known about, he'll do anything to protect them—even employ the brutal skills that have no place in civilized society.

Devon Reese—She returns to her hometown for peace and quiet when a neighbor is murdered and her son withdraws after the crime. But the killer follows her, suspecting she's an eyewitness, and she must turn to the man she'd written off as dead, who's now a stranger, to protect her and their son.

Michael Roarke—The murder of his grandmotherly neighbor sends the little boy into a private world of fear. What he's not telling his mother might end up getting them both killed.

Mrs. Del Vecchio—This quirky senior citizen had a special relationship with Michael Roarke, but her murder winds up putting the boy in danger.

Johnny Del—Mrs. Del Vecchio's dead husband was the leader of a gang of bank robbers. Does his criminal past cast a long shadow over the present?

Dr. Elena Estrada—This psychiatrist tries to help Michael come out of his shell...and puts herself in danger for her efforts.

Sam Frost—Dr. Estrada's new boyfriend is friendly and helpful, but what does she really know about his past?

Bud "The Pelican" Pelicano—One of Johnny Del's old cohorts, he died in prison, but may have lived long enough to pass off the secrets of his criminal past to his son.

Mayor Tyler Davis—He's all about projecting a pristine image of Coral Cove to attract tourists, and he doesn't appreciate the fact that big-city crime has followed Devon to his town. How far will he go to get her to leave?

Chapter One

Devon Reese stopped dead in her tracks. She balanced the laundry basket on her hip and tilted her head, listening for a second thump from downstairs. Either Mrs. Del Vecchio had just knocked something over or the eighty-year-old widow had taken up aerobics.

Hearing only street noises from her North Beach neighborhood in San Francisco wafting through the open window, Devon hitched up the basket and pushed the bathroom door wide. She plucked her towel from the rack and swept up Michael's towel from the floor. She tossed a few washcloths into the basket and then gripped the handles.

She tiptoed past the closed door of Michael's room where he was napping, and padded into the kitchen on bare feet. Crouching down, she grabbed a bottle of detergent from under the sink and then dumped some quarters into her palm. Devon dreaded laundry day, especially since she had to haul down to the ground floor for the laundry room.

She snagged her keys from the hook by the door. Once in the hallway, she turned to lock the deadbolt. Even as a single mom, she felt safe in their building with the security door in the front. But she never left Michael alone in an unlocked apartment, even for the five minutes it took to load the laundry in the washing machine.

Jogging down the stairs, Devon clutched the basket of towels to her chest and peered over the top. She hit the bottom step and crossed the hall in front of Mrs. Del Vecchio's door. Maybe she should check up on the old gal. That thump could've meant a bad fall. She owed her that since Mrs. Del Vecchio had taken a particular interest in Michael, baking him cookies and telling him interesting, if unusual, stories about cops and robbers and pirates.

Devon peeked in at the silent machines in the laundry room and grinned. "It's my lucky day."

Sad but true that a couple of empty washing machines ranked up there as one of the highlights of her day off from the hospital. Since she'd lost her fiancé and given birth to their son alone, she'd learned to find joy in the smallest pleasures of life.

As she loaded her towels, the door to the laundry room slammed shut. She jumped and spun around with her heart pounding. Lunging for the door, she swung it open and peered into the hallway just in time to see the security door to the building click shut.

Probably that annoying kid in the corner apartment upstairs. Last week he kept practicing skateboard jumps off the front steps of the apartment house.

Devon kicked down the door stopper and returned to the washing machine. She dumped her detergent into the receptacle and punched the buttons for a warm-water wash.

As she left the laundry room, she nearly bumped into Sharon Mosely, mother of the obnoxious teen. "Oops, excuse me, Sharon. Hey, did your son just come this way?"

Sharon squeezed past Devon with her own basket. "No. He's at the skate park. Sorry for the incident on the steps last week. Just wait until your little one is a teenager. Enjoy him while he's young and sweet."

Devon rolled her eyes. "I plan to."

She passed Mrs. Del Vecchio's door and then backtracked. Pressing her ear against the panel, she tapped lightly. "Mrs. Del Vecchio?"

Silence.

Devon knocked louder. "Mrs. Del Vecchio, are you in there? Are you okay?"

Holding her breath, Devon grasped the door handle and knocked again. It was a huge ordeal for Mrs. Del Vecchio to venture outside, so she had to be home. Besides, hadn't Devon just heard a big thump from her apartment?

She twisted the door handle and let out a breath when it turned in her hand. Bumping the door with her hip, Devon called, "Mrs. Del Vecchio?"

The sound of running water filled the small apartment along with the overpowering scent of lemon. Drawing her brows over her nose, Devon crept farther into the room.

A couple of sofa pillows lay scattered on the floor. A desk drawer gaped open, its contents littering the carpet. Books tilted helter-skelter on a built-in shelf.

Devon folded her arms, her fingers pinching into her biceps. A chill inched its way up her spine with each step into the disordered apartment. "Mrs. Del Vecchio?"

Devon followed the sound of the water coming from the kitchen. She reached the kitchen entryway and grabbed on to the doorjamb for support as she gasped and swayed forward.

Mrs. Del Vecchio's body lay in a crumpled heap on the tiled floor. Water flowed over the lip of the sink and streamed down the cabinets, creating a pool of bubbles where the lemon-scented dishwashing liquid dripped.

With her heart racing, Devon peeled her hands

from the doorjamb and stumbled toward Mrs. Del Vecchio. She must have slipped and fallen, but how did her entire head get wet?

And why was her apartment a mess?

Devon's training as a nurse kicked in, and she willed her legs to stop trembling. She knelt in the soapy water and brushed away the damp gray strands of hair clinging to Mrs. Del Vecchio's neck to check her pulse.

"Mrs. Del Vecchio!" She didn't figure her neighbor was conscious, but she had to make sure.

Mrs. Del Vecchio's head lolled to the side and Devon gritted her teeth. The old woman's eyes were wide open and her skin had a bluish tinge. She hadn't fallen and hit her head.

Devon's gaze darted to the sink overflowing with water and back to Mrs. Del Vecchio's neck, where red welts were beginning to turn purple. She slid Mrs. Del Vecchio onto her back, tilted her chin up, and pumped her chest. She paused, pressing her ear against her neighbor's heart.

A woman screamed behind her, and Devon's head shot up. Sharon sagged in the doorway to the kitchen, a white-knuckled fist pressed against her mouth.

"Sharon, call 911. I don't know if there's anything I can do for her."

Even though Devon was an obstetrics nurse,

she knew death when she saw it. But what kind of death? Strangulation? Drowning? Both?

However Mrs. Del Vecchio died, it was no accident.

SQUEEZING HER SON'S clammy hand, Devon glanced over her right shoulder at the white van that had rolled into the coastal lookout area and parked next to her car. Her heart lurched painfully as she bent toward Michael's dark head.

"It's okay now, sweetie. We're home. Bad things don't happen in Coral Cove."

Devon sealed her lie with a kiss on Michael's sun-drenched hair. Even though her hometown of Coral Cove had endured its share of tragedies, it had always seemed like a safe refuge—until those murders last month. But the killer had died, the tourists were back for a summer of sun and surf, and it sure beat the heck out of San Francisco in the safety department.

Her son responded by gripping her hand even tighter and nestling his body against her side. Devon sighed and ruffled Michael's curls. The instant she'd discovered Mrs. Del Vecchio's dead body two weeks ago, Devon had known it would hit her son hard. Mrs. Del Vecchio had been like a grandmother to Michael, a wacky grandmother, but a grandmother nonetheless.

But Devon didn't realize the murder would devastate him, altering his personality from outgoing little boy to this nervous, withdrawn stranger.

She swung her silent son's hand and skipped, hoping to inject a little enthusiasm into his demeanor. "I'm taking you to one of my favorite places in Coral Cove."

When her statement failed to elicit a question from Michael, she continued, forcing a cheery note into her voice. "It's the oldest house in Coral Cove and it even has a name. Columbella House."

Devon pointed to the cliff around the next bend. "The house overlooks the ocean, and there's a path to the beach just before we reach the house. Do you want to go down to the beach?"

Michael nodded and Devon released a breath. The family therapist they'd seen in San Francisco had told Devon to give Michael time to recover from the shock. Devon figured he'd have a better chance of doing that away from their apartment in San Francisco where he'd woken up from his nap just in time to see Mrs. Del Vecchio's body wheeled out beneath a white sheet.

Devon led Michael along the familiar curve of the road, their sneakers scuffing against the sand and gravel on the shoulder. She didn't dare tell Michael that most of the residents of Coral Cove thought Columbella House was haunted. A month ago her son's eyes would've widened at that pronouncement and he would've begged to explore.

Now—her gaze shifted to Michael's stiff, little face as she swallowed hard—he'd freak out.

"There's Columbella House. Nobody lives there now, so I don't think anyone will mind if we use the private access to the beach."

She glanced back at the lookout. A silver sedan had joined her car and the van. Maybe they were waiting for the sunset.

The little wooden gate that opened onto the path to the beach squeaked as Devon unhitched it and pulled it toward her, a piece of rotten wood breaking off in her hand. She jerked her head up and narrowed her eyes at the shuttered windows on the second story of the house.

The hair on the back of her neck quivered, but the windows stared back at her blankly. Sweeping her hand across her sweatshirt, she grimaced. Michael's skittishness had infected her—that and the fact that the police suspected Mrs. Del Vecchio's killer was the one who slammed shut the laundry room door on his way out of the building.

No need to feel nervous here. Columbella House had never felt menacing to her. She was probably one of the few people left in Coral Cove who cherished fond memories of the house. One of the few people left *alive* who cherished fond memories.

Rubbing the back of her hand across her tingling nose, she grabbed Michael's wrist. "The path's not too steep, but be careful. I think Coral

Cove had a lot of rain this past spring. It makes the ground spongy."

Michael twisted from her hold and clambered down the path ahead of her. Her son may have lost his desire to speak, but the trauma of Mrs. Del Vecchio's murder hadn't curtailed his agility and natural athletic ability. He'd gotten those attributes from his dad.

Devon picked her way down the rocky trail. The sound of a car's engine caused her to twist her head around, but she could no longer see the road. Not many tourists ventured this way since the Private Property sign discouraged interlopers, and the locals generally steered clear of Columbella House. Still, the lookout point attracted some tourists, like the inhabitants of that white van and the sedan, and the summer season had already drawn its share of people to Coral Cove. Already, the small town boasted a good number of tourists...and strangers.

She hoped the cozy atmosphere here would have a healing effect on Michael. She jumped as a rock rolled past her foot. God knows, Coral Cove hadn't done much to soothe *her* yet. Too many memories.

Michael had scrambled off the last of the boulders that tumbled to the dry sand. Devon called, "Wait right there."

Shading her eyes against the sun low on the

horizon, Devon squinted at the glassy waves scurrying onto the shore. The tide remained low, but she remembered how the water could rush in suddenly, soaking beach towels and carrying sand toys out to sea.

She tromped down the remainder of the path, and then perched on a rock next to Michael. "Pretty cool, huh? I bet you don't remember it here."

After her dad had passed away, Devon and her twin brother, Dylan, had come back to Coral Cove for the funeral. Michael had been two then. Dylan was already working as a cop for the San Jose P.D., following in his dad's footsteps. Their father had been the police chief of Coral Cove for years, and their mom couldn't live here anymore without him. Guess Devon had sort of followed in her mom's footsteps since Coral Cove hadn't been as welcoming to her since her fiancé had disappeared.

"Do you want to do some exploring before the sun goes down?" Devon pushed up from the rock and extended her hand to Michael.

He nodded but brushed her hand aside as he jumped from the rock, immediately scooping up smaller pebbles from the sand.

Devon shoved her hands into the front pocket of her sweatshirt, twisting her fingers together.

Michael's small show of independence had to be a good sign.

Scuffing along the dry sand, Devon kept an eye on her son as he took a zigzag route toward the sea cave at the end of the beach, his ubiquitous blue backpack bouncing against his back. Surely time would heal his shock over what had happened to Mrs. Del Vecchio.

The SFPD had ruled Mrs. Del Vecchio's death a murder. The autopsy had confirmed death by drowning. The welts on her neck had been where her killer had grabbed her, forcing her head into the kitchen sink filled with water.

Devon crossed her arms, hunching her shoulders. Why would someone murder an eighty-year-old woman like that? As far as the cops could tell, the killer hadn't stolen anything from the apartment even though it had been ransacked. The murder had spooked enough of the residents that several of them had taken extended vacations—including Devon. She'd taken a leave of absence from the hospital.

Now she just wanted her son back.

Michael hesitated at the mouth of the cave, twisting his head over his shoulder.

"It's okay. I'll come with you." Devon jogged across the sand and grabbed Michael's hand. This time he returned the pressure and they ducked into the cave together.

The waves crashing against the walls of the cave created an echoing bass sound that made Devon's chest tingle. The moist walls dripped salt water on their heads and Devon inhaled the briny scent.

Michael squatted next to a tide pool, almost dipping his nose in the water.

"It's hard to see in here this time of day, but we'll come back one morning." She jerked her thumb toward a small opening at the top of a pile of rocks. "Do you want to climb up there and peek through the little window?"

Like a mountain goat, Michael scampered up the rocks and shoved his head into the opening in the side of the cave, which seemed bigger than Devon had remembered it. Time, wind and sea water had done their part to erode the rock.

Michael thrust his entire head and shoulders through the hole and Devon sucked in a sharp breath. "Come out of there, Michael."

By the time Devon placed one foot on the first level of rock, Michael's upper torso, backpack and all, had disappeared. "Michael!" Her voice bounced off the walls of the cave, merging with the deep booming.

The opening became a living entity sucking Michael's body farther into its depths. Devon knew only more rocks and a sheer drop into a rough sea awaited Michael on the other side of that hole.

As Michael's legs wriggled through the opening, Devon screamed, flinging her hands in front of her in a desperate but empty move to grab him. She couldn't fit through that hole. Her only hope of saving her son was to exit the cave and circle around on top of it…and valuable seconds were ticking away.

She jumped from the rocks, her feet landing in a pool of water. She sloshed her way out of the cave, her chest heaving with sobs, incoherent prayers tumbling from her lips.

Stumbling from the cave, she blinked in the light and lurched toward the boulders scattered up the incline toward the road. She banged her knee as she clambered on top of the first rock.

"Michael!" She crawled onto the next rock and craned her neck to get a clear view of the top of the cave. Her teeth chattered and her hands shook as she gazed at the empty expanse of rock.

Oh, God, he must've fallen into the water.

Devon staggered to her feet, flinging her arms out for balance. Adrenaline pumped through her body. She'd make it to the edge of the rock and then she'd jump in to save him.

"He's here. He's safe."

Clasping her hands to her chest where her thundering heart threatened to burst through, Devon spun around toward the male voice. A tall man with windswept black hair had one hand clamped on Michael's shoulder.

Devon ran her tongue around her dry lips and swallowed. The relief weakened her knees and she sank to the ground.

Michael struggled against the man's hold, and Devon realized he was keeping her son off the dangerous rocks. But Michael didn't like strangers…not anymore.

Devon scooped the salty air into her lungs and rose to her feet. "It's okay, Michael. Stay with the man. I'm coming."

She straightened her spine and on trembling legs, she strode toward her son and the stranger who had saved him. The man's long hair blew back from his face, a black patch covering one eye.

Great. Before Mrs. Del Vecchio's murder, Michael would've pegged the man as a pirate and would've been as excited as all get-out. Now he'd view him as another scary stranger.

Devon jumped from the rocks to the sand and her step faltered. The way the man held his head. His lean muscular frame. She drew closer. The set of his jaw. Her steps quickened. The black, black hair like a velvet midnight sky.

She choked and tripped. She extended her arms like a blind woman, no, like a woman staggering through the desert toward an oasis.

When she fully focused on the man's face, Devon fell to her knees, crying out in indescribable shock and joy.

Her fiancé, Kieran Roarke, had come back from the dead.

Chapter Two

Kieran dug his long fingers into the boy's bony shoulder. Was his mother injured? Relieved to see her son?

Or had she just seen a ghost?

The squirming boy broke away from his grasp and flew to the woman still kneeling on the ground. Holding the boy against his will had pained Kieran. He had frightened the boy when he'd plucked him from those rocks and carried him down to the sand, but he'd probably saved him from a tumble over the edge and into the sea.

Maybe he should've allowed the other man making his way toward the boy a chance to save him. He turned, but the man had disappeared.

Kieran had been watching them—the boy and his mother. He'd been watching them for a few days and knew the woman would come to Columbella House. Just as Kieran, through the foggy memories of his messed-up mind, had been drawn to this small town and the house looming over the sea, the woman had been lured here as well. He'd recognized the woman as soon as he'd seen her on the street—recognized her from his dreams.

When the ethereal blonde had dropped to the ground, Kieran's first response had been to rush to her rescue. But when she looked up at him, she was laughing…crying…laughing and crying at the same time.

Now she stumbled to her feet, gripping the little boy's hand, a smile of pure joy lighting her beautiful face. She reached her other hand out to him and breathed his name. "Kieran."

Pain sliced through his head, pooling in his damaged eye. Gritting his teeth, he rode it out, allowing the memories to crisscross his brain. He'd heard his name on her lips many times before—in laughter, in anger, in desire. He tried to focus, but as usual, the strands of his life floated away out of reach.

"Are you okay?" He took a step forward.

Her eyes widened and a haze of confusion shifted across her face. "A-am I okay? I thought you were dead."

Did she expect him to sweep her into his arms? Assure her he'd never leave her again? Shoving his hands in his pockets, he dug his heels into the grains of sand littering the rock. He couldn't do that—not now, not ever.

After he'd escaped from that hellhole in Afghanistan and made it to safety, the army had sent him to a hospital in Germany. They'd told him his name and a few other basics, but then the military sent him to Walter Reed. They wanted to debrief him in the States and scheduled him to see an army psychiatrist to help him regain his memory.

But he'd had enough of people telling him what to do.

Kieran squared his shoulders and took a deep breath of moist, salty air. "I don't know who you are."

Her face crumpled and she looked ready to pitch forward.

He had to do better than that. He dragged his hands out of his pockets and held them out in supplication.

"I have some memory, but some things...I have jolts or flashes. I know you," he clenched his fist and pounded it against his chest, "here, but I don't know who you are. I don't know your name."

She covered her mouth with one hand as silent tears dripped from her eyes and streamed across her fingers. Wiping her hand across her nose, she drew in a shuddering breath. "I'm Devon. Devon Reese. I'm your... We were engaged."

Kieran squeezed his good eye closed and whispered her name. "Devon. Devon."

Yes, the name filled him with warmth and longing, those feelings belonged to his hazy past. They *were* engaged. A woman like Devon, filled with golden light and promise, would never want a damaged man like him.

Maybe she'd already moved on. The boy had to have a father somewhere. And if she hadn't already moved on, Kieran would make sure she did.

Soft fingers traced the edge of his eye patch, and he jerked back. She'd moved across the sand silently, tugging the quiet boy in her wake. He looked into her tear-streaked face and had to drag his gaze away from the luminous depths of her blue eyes before he drowned. He didn't have time for weakness, the kind of weakness that had drawn him to this place and this woman. For four long years he'd expunged every kind of weakness from his soul…or his captors had beaten it out of him.

"What happened to your eye?"

He scanned her voice for an ounce of pity. Finding none, he shrugged. "I don't remember."

The ocean breeze tousled Devon's blond mane, and she grabbed it with one hand, pulling it back from her face. "Can we continue this conversation up top? The tide's going to be moving in soon."

Kieran wanted to continue talking to Devon. He wanted to continue basking in her glow. He wanted to get answers. He knew the conversation would end in heartache for her, but his years imprisoned in that filthy hovel had taught him self-ishness. It had given him a brittle heart.

"Sure." He pointed to the boy who had been clinging to Devon's leg throughout their exchange. "Is your son okay?"

Devon's cheeks flushed bright red. "Michael's fine."

Touchy subject? He didn't know much about kids, but the boy didn't seem fine to him.

Kieran climbed over the first set of boulders and turned to give Devon and her son a hand, but they had navigated the rocks with ease. Even the boy, who had seemed tentative and withdrawn, was scampering across the rocks like his feet knew every step.

"This is the easiest path back up to the road." Devon jerked her thumb over her shoulder. "Or do you remember that?"

Kieran knew it but not because he remembered it from years ago. He knew it because he'd been hiding out at Columbella House...waiting for Devon.

He said, "I know," and swept his arm in front of him. "Why don't you two go ahead?"

Hoisting herself up onto his rock, Devon squeezed past him. Her silky hair brushed his shoulder and he inhaled her intoxicating scent—all sweetness and purity. Who needed food and water? That smell alone could sustain him for years.

Kieran clenched his jaw. *Stop dreaming, Roarke. You're on a fact-finding mission. And that's it.*

As Devon climbed ahead of him, Kieran's gaze traced the outline of her body beneath her baggy sweatshirt and cargo shorts. His fingertips tingled with the remembrance of her smooth skin. Since he'd lost his memory, his senses had taken up where his mind had left off. Smells, sounds and touches could trigger responses from him even if he couldn't remember the occasions that elicited those responses.

Maybe he should've continued with his debriefing and psychiatric help, but he didn't want the army implanting any memories that didn't belong there or messing with the ones that did. He knew how the black-ops division of the military conducted business. Hadn't they told his brother he was dead? Hadn't they refused to contact his brother or parents when he'd been found alive? Military security. National security. Top secret information. He'd heard it all before.

Of course, nothing stopped him from contacting his family now. But what would they want with him? Apparently, his younger brother, Colin, had escaped from the same captors that had held Kieran against his will for four long years. His brother had probably moved on with his life. He wouldn't want to be reminded of what he'd endured, especially by a man who had no memories, a man whose very soul had turned black with rage.

Devon slipped and skidded toward him. Kieran caught her around the waist, steadying her. "Careful."

She looked down at him, her moist lips slightly parted, her blue eyes bright with tears. His hand tightened as his breath came out in short spurts. He shouldn't have come here. Why subject Devon to his presence when he'd spared his brother and parents?

Her golden lashes fluttered, and his heart skittered in his chest. Weakness. That's what led him here in the first place. He couldn't succumb to it. Ever. If he had shown any weakness to his captors, they would've killed him.

He dropped his hands from Devon's waist as if he'd been scorched. She blinked twice, turned and continued to hike up the path to the road.

When they reached the top, Devon faced him with her hands on her hips. "Have you contacted anyone else in Coral Cove? Do you know you have a brother…Colin? There are people, other people who have been devastated by your—" she glanced at her son "—disappearance."

"Let's get off the side of the road." He jerked his head toward Columbella House. "I've been bunking there. We can talk on the deck."

Devon's brows shot up. "You've been staying at Columbella House? Do you know that you have a house down the road? Or rather the house belongs to your parents. You grew up there."

"I didn't know that." He shrugged. He'd figured he'd grown up in Coral Cove, but no other house or location in this town had drawn him like this one. "Is Colin still here?"

"No. Coincidentally, he was in town last month, investigating…investigating." Devon waved her hands in the air.

Kieran unlatched the gate leading to the back of the house and a wooden deck that perched over the rocks. Nobody from the street could see this deck and Kieran had brushed off the Adirondack chairs and enjoyed several sunsets from this vantage point.

"Have a seat." He nudged one chair with his foot. Grabbing a wicker basket from the corner, he said, "Michael, do you want to look at some cool shells?"

The boy ignored him, but slid a gaze toward his mother. "Can I find a Columbella?"

"Maybe." She flicked her fingers toward the basket. "Have a look."

Michael slipped his backpack from his shoulders and placed it next to the basket. As he sat cross-legged in front of the basket and pulled out the first shell, Devon seemed to melt into the chair.

Something about the boy was off. Of course, Kieran didn't know Michael at all and he might have judged him a little shy or clingy except for the tension that stiffened Devon's body whenever she looked at her son.

"So I grew up in Coral Cove and we were engaged."

Devon's attention snapped back to him as she sucked in a quick breath.

He'd have to work on his social skills if he hoped to have a life in the free world. His tormenters hadn't valued the attributes of subtlety or nuance.

"Yes, but not in high school." She drew up her knees, wrapping her arms around her legs. "We reconnected when we both returned home after graduating from college. I was planning on going to nursing school, and you were going into the military. You had a thing for languages. Do you...?"

"Do I still speak several languages?" Kieran gripped the flat arms of the chair. "Yeah. I didn't forget the languages, just the rest of my life."

Devon balanced her chin on her knees, watching Michael. "What happened, Kieran? Can you at least tell me that?"

"A military operation that went south."

"Colin was with you, but he was with the FBI." Kieran's eye twitched beneath his patch. "It was a multi-task force raid on a terrorist group, but someone snitched us off. I don't remember much about it. The army briefed me after I escaped."

"H-how long?" She rolled her head to the side, resting her cheek on her knee as her blond hair swept across her legs.

He knew just how the strands would feel slipping through his fingers. He raked his hair back from his face and said, "Four years."

She gasped and choked. "You were in some kind of prison for four years?"

"Some kind of prison. Not nearly as nice as what we have going on here." His lips twisted in a bitter smile. A filthy cot. An earthenware pot for a toilet. Stale bread for dinner. And the beatings, always the beatings.

He'd never tell Devon any of that. She belonged light years away from all of it. Light years away from him.

She closed her eyes and a tear slid from beneath her lashes. "I'm so sorry, Kieran. You lost your memory while you were imprisoned? Everything? Every memory?"

Almost every memory except for a golden warmth that kept him alive.

"I think I took a particularly bad blow to the head during some kind of beating." He pointed to his patch. "Probably when that happened. When I came to, I could piece together that I was military and that I was a prisoner of war. Certain memories would float in and out."

Devon looked up, a tear trembling on the edge of her lashes. "But no memories of me?"

How could he explain it to her? He couldn't remember her face or her name, or even that he had a fiancée. But every day in that damned prison he had a will to survive, some force of goodness and light that shored up his strength, hardened him against the torture, forged a brutal desire to live.

Left a shell of a man.

How ironic that he now had to give up the source of his survival because the survival itself had turned him into a monster.

His jaw tightened. "No. No memories of you."

The soft sigh from her lips made him clench his hands and turn his gaze onto the boy, patiently sorting shells, examining each one as if looking for a pearl.

"Then why are you here? Shouldn't you be in treatment or something?" She brushed her hair from her face and straightened her spine, pinning her shoulders to the back of the chair.

Kieran shrugged. "The army wanted to send me to some shrink at Walter Reed. I chose not to go. I want to recover my memories in my own way, in my own time."

"But surely the army told you about your brother

and the location of your parents? They must've told you about growing up in Coral Cove."

The army had told him all of that, but the minute Lieutenant Jeffries, his debriefer, had mentioned Coral Cove, Kieran knew he had to come here first. He knew he'd find his guardian angel in Coral Cove, and as soon as he'd spotted Devon his soul had recognized her. The familiar feelings of hope and optimism had flooded his senses.

"The army also told my parents and my brother that I was dead. They haven't bothered to notify them otherwise since I was on a top secret mission, even though Colin was on that same mission. I came here first because I wanted to ease into things slowly." The lie of his last statement came to his lips easily. He'd perfected lying over the past few years—lying and a lot of other skills that had no place in a civilized society. No place in Devon's life.

Devon peered at him in the encroaching darkness and whispered, "Do you want me to help you?"

"Yes." The word flew from his lips before he had time to swallow it. "No. I don't want you to go to any trouble."

Her eyes widened, and then she tilted her head back and laughed. She doubled over and laughed some more, her shoulders shaking. When she raised her head, strands of hair clung to her wet cheeks. Her laughter continued unabated, but she didn't have a smile on her beautiful face.

Michael studied his mother with a frown crinkling his face and clutching two shells in his hands. Even he recognized that her laughter was bereft of humor.

"Go to any trouble?" She wiped the back of her hand across her nose and hiccupped. "We were engaged, Kieran. You disappeared from my life, and then Colin told me you were dead. I was devastated. I could barely get out of bed in the morning. I could barely drag myself into work. I couldn't envision my life without you. I felt dead."

Her words punched him in the gut, adding to his guilt and rage that he hadn't escaped his captors sooner. "I'm sorry, Devon."

He gazed at Michael, who had gone back to his game with the shells when his mother had stopped laughing. Devon had gone on. Had met someone else. Reclaimed her life. That little boy was evidence of that.

"Don't be sorry." Devon gathered her blond hair and twisted it around her hand like a golden rope. "It was fate, just like running into you in Coral Cove on my escape from the city."

Escape? What was she running from? Unease crawled across his flesh. He slid a look at Michael. Where was his father?

Kieran inhaled the sea air and expelled it between his clenched teeth. "Was that Michael's father on the cliff? Is that why you were so worried?"

"What?" Her brow furrowed as she tilted her head. "Was who Michael's father?"

"The man in the white van on the cliff. The man watching Michael."

THE WHITE VAN.

Kieran's words sliced through the fog swirling around her brain. Too many discoveries had pummeled her in such a short period of time, her mind was still reeling. For a minute, she'd thought Kieran had asked about Michael's father.

She remembered the white van in the lookout area. "There was someone watching Michael when he came up on the rocks?"

Kieran's shoulders relaxed. "I—I saw you and Michael climb down to the beach. A man had gotten out of the van and was standing at the edge of the lookout. I thought he was making a move toward Michael when he clambered out of the cave, but I got to the boy first."

Devon shrugged, but a finger of fear had touched the back of her neck. Why had she even noticed that van? She'd been on edge ever since Mrs. Del Vecchio's murder.

But now she had bigger issues on her plate. Kieran didn't even remember her. She hadn't had a chance to tell him about her pregnancy before he'd left for Afghanistan on that top secret mission.

Should she give him some time to piece together the fragments of his life before springing paternity on him? She glanced at the dark stranger coiled in the deck chair, the black patch hiding one eye and a guarded secrecy hiding the other.

Hugging herself, she rubbed her arms. "The guy in the van was a stranger. I'm not running from Michael's father if that's what you're thinking."

At least not yet.

"That's good." He tilted his chin toward her. "Are you cold? Should we continue this conversation inside?"

He couldn't even bring himself to touch her. What had those monsters done to him?

"Inside Columbella?" She glanced at Michael, whose hands had stalled above the shells.

"It's shelter from the breeze, anyway."

"Have you actually been staying in the house?"

"It's the only place I remembered."

"H-have you been to the burned-out room?" Did he remember that room? It had been their secret place.

"I saw a room off the library that was scorched." He threw a sidelong glance at Michael. "It seemed…"

"There was a fire there last month." She scooted up to the edge of her chair. "I have a better idea."

His frame stiffened and he clutched the arms of the chair as if ready for takeoff. "What?"

"Your parents have a perfectly good house across the street." She waved her arm in the general direction of the street on the other side of Columbella House. "It has electricity and everything."

"Is it occupied?"

Kieran didn't want to see his family? Yes, he was a different man.

"No. Your parents live in Hawaii now, and Colin just left. He'd been staying there while he was in town." She crooked her finger at a sleepy Michael, rubbing his eyes, and patted her lap.

"Where's Colin now?"

Devon scooped Michael into her lap, and he tucked his head into the hollow of her neck. His dark lashes fluttered on his cheeks and Devon's heart skipped a beat. Couldn't Kieran see his mirror image in Michael?

"I don't know. I asked, but apparently Colin took off with Michelle Girard. Do you remember her? She lived…" She trailed off as Kieran shook his head. "Anyway, they took off for parts unknown."

Kieran rubbed his knuckles against the black stubble of his beard. "People are going to know me here, aren't they?"

Devon allowed her mouth to hang open for a

few seconds. "Of course. I don't understand how you've avoided detection up until this point."

"I haven't been here long and I haven't been out much. The town's already clogged with tourists. What's one more with a baseball cap pulled over his face?"

"You're one of Coral Cove's favorite sons, Kieran. High school football star, football scholarship to college, prestigious language institute before joining the Green Berets." She brushed a hand across Michael's smooth cheek, taking note of his measured breathing, and whispered, "People think you're dead."

His one dark eye glittered, unfathomable beneath a half-mast lid. "I suppose I'd cause a stir if I hit the streets."

"*If* you hit the streets? You're not staying?" Her hands bunched Michael's T-shirt as she hugged his sleeping form closer to her body. "Y-you need medical treatment. Psychiatric treatment."

"I can get that at Walter Reed."

"I thought you didn't trust the government."

"Is that what you're doing here?"

"What?" She wasn't sure she liked this abrupt-talking stranger with the piercing eyes...eye. Was he blind beneath that patch?

He leveled a finger at Michael. "What's wrong with your boy?"

Devon hunched over Michael's body in a protective gesture. Was it so clear that Michael had issues? Or was Kieran extra perceptive because of his half blindness...or because he was Michael's father?

"What do you mean?"

"He's what? Five? Six? He's not very vocal. He's jumpy. Uneasy. Watchful."

Like his father.

"He's four." Devon held her breath, waiting for Kieran to start calculating the years in his head. Did he even remember the last time they were together? Probably not if he thought Michael could be six years old.

Devon slumped in her chair. "Our downstairs neighbor was murdered last month. Michael hasn't been the same since."

"Murder can be tough for a kid to handle. Did he know her well?"

"They were...close. But I never told Michael Mrs. Del Vecchio was murdered, just that she had died."

"Maybe he found out."

"I don't know. He won't talk about it." Her nose tingled with tears and she buried her face in Michael's soft hair.

"Is he in treatment?"

"He was seeing a therapist in the city, but I wanted to get away from our apartment house. The therapist thought it was a good idea, too."

"And now?"

"This is my hometown, a refuge." Or at least it was before her dead fiancé showed up with no memory. "There also happens to be a great therapist here, who works with hypnosis. She's a family friend, too, so I trust her with Michael."

"Hypnosis, huh?"

"She could probably help you, too, Kieran. She's a family therapist—sees both kids and adults." She needed another way to keep him here in Coral Cove besides the obvious. Once she told him about Michael, would he feel obligated to stay and try to work things out? The man already had enough pressure.

"Maybe." He stretched his long legs in front of him and his arms over his head. "Your little one is out. You should get him to bed."

She peered at the sun dipping into the ocean, one orange crescent floating on a dark blue ripple. "It's dinner time. He's going to have to wake up to eat."

Kieran pushed up from his chair and crossed to hers in two long steps. He held out his arms. "Do you want me to carry him back to your car?"

"I have a better idea. Your parents' place is just down the street, and I know where they keep the key."

She shifted, and Kieran bent over, arms still outstretched to take Michael.

"Are you sure?"

"Are *you* sure? Will he freak out if he wakes up and I'm carrying him?"

Devon gulped. *Maybe not if he knew you were his father.*

"He's a pretty heavy sleeper. I think he'll be okay."

Kieran slid his arms beneath Michael's body, one under his back and the other behind his knees. Devon released her son to his father for the first time ever.

Straightening, Kieran hoisted Michael in his arms and secured him against his broad chest.

Devon blinked her eyes and dipped her head, allowing her hair to create a veil over her face. She had to tell him. The knowledge might mess with his mind even more, but it might help him, give him something to live for…because she wasn't enough for him anymore.

"Lead the way."

The fact that she was guiding Kieran to his parents' house created another level of unreality to this day. Why had Columbella House imprinted itself on his memory instead of his family home? A tiny flame of hope flickered in her chest. Was it because of her? Because of what they'd shared in that house, in that now burned-out room?

She held the side gate open for Kieran and Michael snug in his arms. "Let's stop at my car first. I want to grab my purse. You can wait here."

"I'll come with you. Michael's as light as a feather."

Their feet crunched the gravel as they walked single file on the road around the bend to the lookout. Her car sat all by itself. The other two people hadn't stayed for the sunset after all.

As she approached her car, she tilted her head. "Why's my car listing to one side?"

Kieran swore. "Because your tires have been slashed."

Chapter Three

Hot anger raced across her skin and she clenched her hands. "Are you kidding me?"

"Your back window is broken, too." Shifting Michael in his arms, Kieran crouched in the broken glass as he peered into the gaping window. "Did they take anything?"

With shaking hands, Devon beeped her remote and yanked open the passenger-side door. Bending over, she felt under the seat for her small handbag. "My purse is gone."

"Did you lose much?"

"Besides my faith in the sanctity of small towns?" She kicked at the pebbles of glass on the ground. "I lost my driver's license and a little cash. Luckily I didn't have my whole wallet in there with all my credit cards and other ID."

"You shouldn't leave your purse in the car like that."

She stamped her foot, scattering bits of her car window. "I hid it under the seat. And why did he have to add insult to injury and slash two of my tires?"

"Maybe to slow your pursuit."

"Yeah, like I'm going to pursue some thief."

"You have to call the cops." He pointed to the floor of her car. "Or was your cell phone in your purse?"

She patted the pocket of her shorts. "Right here. If I call the cops and they find you here, you're going to cause a sensation. Are you ready for that?"

He shrugged. "Where would I go?"

"Go to your folks' house, and take Michael with you." She brushed a strand of brown hair from Michael's forehead. "I don't want him waking up and finding the cops. I don't want him to see my car."

"And I don't want to leave you here on your own, especially after this." He jerked his head toward the mess of her car.

"I'll be fine." She'd tried but couldn't quash the tremor in her voice. She didn't want to stand out on the road waiting for the cops, either. "But if you insist, you can watch me from the corner of Columbella House until the cops come and then I'll have them drop me off at your parents' house."

"Uh, where is my parents' house, and what if Michael wakes up while you're gone?"

"I'd rather Michael be a little frightened by

someone he's already talked to than have him see the police again and the condition of this car."

She told Kieran how to get to his own house and told him where his parents kept the key. Then she called the cops.

Kieran retreated to the edge of Columbella House with Michael secure in his arms. The two of them looked so natural together she almost smiled, even though neither knew the other's identity.

She'd have to remedy that…and soon.

When one Coral Cove police unit pulled up to the lookout, lights flashing, Devon knew she'd made the right decision to send Michael off with his father. Out of the corner of her eye, she saw the two of them slip into the shadows.

A young officer swung out of the patrol car, hand on his holster as if he expected to find the suspect, knife in hand. Of course, the police were probably still on edge after the murders last month, even though the perpetrator had died in that fire at Columbella.

"Devon Reese, is that you?"

"Clark?" She recognized the officer now. He'd been a few years behind her in school. "Wow, you're a cop now."

"Yeah, too bad your dad's not chief anymore." His cheeks reddened. "Not that I don't like Chief Evans."

"I heard Chief Evans might be leaving. That's what my brother told me anyway, and he's interested in the job."

"That'd be great to have another Chief Reese in town." He aimed his finger at her car. "What happened? I can't believe any kids are responsible for this. Do you think it could've been a tourist? A stranger passing through?"

Her mind flitted to the white van. Is that why the man had been watching Michael? To make sure he had time to steal her purse?

"I don't know. I saw a silver sedan and a white van parked next to my car when Mi… I went down to the beach."

"Did you get a plate?"

"No."

Clark tried to lift some prints from the car, but it didn't look like he was having much luck. He took down a description of her purse and the cars and told her to get a car alarm installed.

"Do you need a tow?"

"I already called Gary's shop in town. He's going to come out and get it. In the meantime, can you drop me off at the Roarkes' house up the street?"

"Sure. You shouldn't be hanging around Columbella House, anyway. My girlfriend said she saw lights in the house the other night."

Kieran's lights?

"I'm glad that fire didn't destroy the whole house."

Clark shook his head. "Maybe it should have. Some around here, including the mayor, want to preserve the house, but I wish the St. Regis twins would just tear it down."

"It's not the house's fault." She slid into the front seat of the patrol car and snapped her seat belt. "I can't believe Larry Brunswick, the algebra teacher, turned out to be the killer of all those women.

"It was crazy, and then he tried to marry Michelle Girard in that house until Colin Roarke saved her."

Clark cruised down Coral Cove Drive and made a U-turn in front of the Roarkes' house. "Is that why you're here?"

"Huh?"

"At the Roarkes'." He jerked his thumb at the window. "Did Colin forget something?"

"Yeah. Yeah, he forgot something." *His brother.* She thanked Clark and scrambled from the car. She hadn't wanted Michael to wake up to her damaged car and a policeman in uniform, but she didn't want him waking up with a stranger, either...even if that stranger was his father.

A lamp burned in the window of the house, but she doubted Kieran had turned it on—too careful for that. Colin must've left it on or the lamp was on a timer.

Clark waited at the curb, so she sifted through the dirt in a planter at the side of the porch. Her fingers traced the edge of the key. Kieran must have put it back.

She brushed off the key and inserted it into the deadbolt, waving at Clark. Swinging the door open, she took a step into the small entryway. She held her breath and peeked around the corner into the living room.

Kieran looked up from his newspaper, an old one that had headlines of the fiery death of Larry Brunswick, the Reunion Killer. "Everything go okay?"

She blew out a breath as she spotted Michael, still sleeping and tucked into the love seat in the corner. "Well, the cop didn't find anything. I told him about the white van."

"Is your car still there?" He folded the paper in his lap.

"For now. Gary's Auto is sending out a tow truck tonight. He'll replace the tires and see if he has a replacement for the window." She dropped into the chair across from Kieran's. "Everything go okay here?"

"Your son didn't wake up and start screaming at the stranger with the eye patch, so yeah."

Kieran pushed up from his chair and wandered

toward Michael. He swept a lock of dark hair from her son's flushed face. "When are you taking him to see your friend the psychiatrist?"

"Probably tomorrow." She folded her arms, bunching her fists against her body. "Do you want to come along?"

He took a turn around the room, settling in front of the mantel. He studied each framed photo of him and his brother as if imprinting it on his memory. Reaching out, he traced his parents' faces with the tip of his finger.

"You remember Colin, don't you?"

He nodded. "He was with me on the assignment when we were captured. And then he escaped."

"He can't forgive himself for that. The fact that he left you behind tore at him."

"I don't blame him for escaping." He stuffed his hands in the pockets of his tight-fitting jeans. "I know he would've tried to come back for me with reinforcements, but my captors moved me. The army told me that much."

"How did you get away, Kieran?" She gripped her hands in front of her, twisting her fingers into knots. Did she really want to know? Did she want to hear how he'd suffered?

He shrugged. "I escaped."

Had he read the ambivalence in her face? If she was going to help him, reclaim him as her own and Michael's father, she needed to step up to the plate. "You don't remember what happened to your eye?"

"Nope."

"Can you see out of it?"

"Not clearly."

"Can I have a look at it?"

"Nope."

She clenched her teeth. Stubborn man. Closing her eyes, she took a deep breath through her nose, her nostrils flaring. "Did the army doctors look at it?"

"They did." He slipped his index finger beneath the string that held the black patch to his head. "They issued me this after cleaning the wound and running some tests."

"Did the tests show anything? Any sensitivity to light?"

"I don't know. I didn't hang around long enough to find out."

"You just checked yourself out of the hospital and took off?"

"It's my life."

"They'll be coming for you."

"Let 'em try."

She blew out an exasperated breath. Had talking to Kieran always been like talking to a wall of steel? She squared her shoulders. "If you want my help, you're going to have to open up a little more."

"I think you're the one who needs to open up."

Her belly flip-flopped and she shot a glance at Michael still sleeping on the love seat. Had Kieran figured it out?

"I'm an open book. What do you want to know about your life?"

"We knew each other in high school."

Hadn't they already gone over this? Her pounding heart shifted into a lower gear and she could breathe again. "Yes, but we didn't date until later. Like I said before, we'd both come back to Coral Cove—I was going into nursing school and you'd just finished at the language institute and had enlisted with the Green Berets."

"But that wasn't my first mission, the one where I was captured."

"No. We were together through a few of your missions."

As they chatted, Kieran's body seemed to relax, one muscle group at a time, until he sank into a chair, his back to the window and the darkening sky. His lean frame, thinner than she'd remembered, slumped against the cushions of the chair.

"Do you recall more now that you're here in Coral Cove? In this house?" *With me?*

He steepled his fingers and peered at her over the top of the juncture. "I do. The memories come slowly. That's why I made my way back here after

I escaped…from the hospital. I wanted to remember slowly, gradually."

"I want to help you remember."

Kieran seemed to sink farther into the chair, the dusk creeping over his shoulder, masking his face.

"You have your own problems right now. You don't need me to burden you with more."

His return had already constituted a problem for her. Something close to anger percolated in her belly. Then she pressed a hand against her stomach. She never in a million years thought she'd consider the return of Kieran—her fiancé, her love, the father of her child—a problem.

She eyed the dark man across from her, his face still, unreadable. If he wouldn't stay for her help, for her, would he stay for his son?

Flinging her hands in front of her, she tried to dissipate the heavy air between them. "It wouldn't be a burden, Kieran. You're halfway to remembering almost everything…halfway to knowing everything about your life."

"I can't pick up where we left off."

His words twisted the knife in her heart, the knife he'd plunged there when he didn't recognize her on the beach. At this point, would he even want to know he's a father?

"I'm not expecting us to pick up where we left off, Kieran. It's been over four years. You've changed. I've changed."

"You've moved on with your life. You thought I was dead."

She nodded, afraid to blink and dislodge the tears burning behind her lids. In truth, she hadn't moved on with her life. She lived and breathed Kieran every day through his son. She hadn't slept with another man in the entire time after Kieran's disappearance. She could hardly drag herself out on a date.

"We all thought you were dead. I—I'm relieved and so happy that you survived."

His lips twisted. "Did I?"

"You're alive."

"I am." He shifted in the chair as if to remind himself. "And you have your whole life ahead of you with your son. Are you married? Divorced?"

Uh-oh.

"No."

Kieran's hands curled around the arms of the chair. "You never married Michael's father?"

"No."

His body stiffened, the relaxed slouch replaced by planes and angles. "Where is he, Michael's father?"

"Don't you know, Kieran?"

"No." He shot to the edge of his seat, his muscles coiled and ready for flight.

"He's sitting across from me. You're Michael's father."

Chapter Four

Her words sucked the air out of Kieran's lungs. He'd seen it coming at him like a runaway train, at first far away on the horizon, a faint light, a wisp of a dream. Then as the reality drew closer and closer, he'd tried to dodge it until he decided to turn and face it head-on.

He sipped in a short breath to test the pain. He gulped in another. He slipped a glance at his...son, now stirring from the makeshift bed where Kieran had placed him with a gentleness he could've sworn he'd forgotten. A gentleness borne from the fact that the boy belonged to her...and now him.

"I'm sorry, Kieran. I didn't mean to break it to you like that."

He trained his eye on Devon, her blond hair gathering the light from the single lamp. Her eyes sparkled with tears. She'd tried to hide her emotion from him all day, but he could see that his reappearance had thrown her into turmoil.

"Sorry?"

"Mommy?" Michael rolled from the love seat and padded toward Devon on bare feet. He crawled into the chair next to her and stared at Kieran.

His son.

Did the boy fear him? He had every right to fear him—a stranger more scarred on the inside than the outside.

"Are you hungry, Michael?" Devon ruffled her son's dark hair, so like his own.

He'd seen the resemblance almost immediately. How could he not? He'd pushed it away, denied it, almost hoped Devon would lie to him and send him on his way.

But Devon didn't lie. He knew that about her. He could always trust Devon.

And now? Could he trust her to do the right thing for her son and keep him away from a damaged man so filled with rage he had no room for love? A man whose civility had been ripped out of him, tortured out of him?

"Yeah, I'm hungry."

She spread her hands. "I suppose Colin didn't leave any food in the house, and I don't think it would be edible after a month, anyway."

Kieran cleared his throat. "You don't have a car."

"Do you?"

He shook his head. You needed a credit card to

rent a car, and all he had were a few pieces of ID from the army. You also needed your full vision.

"How'd you get to Coral Cove?"

"Planes, buses." He held up his thumb. "Car."

"What have you been eating? Because I know Columbella doesn't have any electricity or gas."

"Fruit, beef jerky, energy bars." He shrugged. "It's a feast compared to what I'm used to."

The air between them sizzled with unasked questions and unspoken words, but Michael's intelligent dark eyes switched from his face to his mother's while they talked.

The boy didn't need any more traumas.

Devon dragged her cell phone out of her pocket and waved it. "We'll call for pizza. I already have the number for Vinnie's on speed dial."

"Does pizza sound good to you, Michael?" Hunching forward, Kieran gripped his knees.

Michael snuggled in close to Devon's body but nodded his head.

One small step.

"Then pizza it is." Devon punched a few keys on her phone. "We're pepperoni fans, Kieran."

She placed an order for two large pepperoni pizzas, salad, garlic bread and soda. Did she think she had to fatten him up? He must look gaunt to her. His appearance in the hospital had shocked him. He would've never been a star football player at this weight. And with one eye.

"Are you sure that's going to be enough food?"

Devon laughed and it sounded like wind chimes tinkling in the breeze. He'd heard those wind chimes many times outside his prison walls, the sound shoring him up, giving him strength.

"Michael eats a lot." She pinched Michael's nose. "At least he used to."

Her bright smile drooped, and Kieran felt as if he'd do anything to bring it back just so he could bask in its warmth.

"Seems like you and I both have some catching up to do in the food department, Michael."

The boy shot him a quick glance beneath a lock of dark hair and Kieran's gut knotted. What was wrong with him? Hearing about the death of a neighbor, even a friendly one, shouldn't have such a strong impact on a kid. Hell, he remembered when his favorite dog died and he'd grieved for about two weeks, which was a week longer than Colin did.

He sucked in a breath. He remembered. He remembered the dog, Duke, and he remembered the day he died.

"Are you okay?"

He glanced up at Devon's face, lines of worry bracketing her mouth. Hell no. He couldn't do this to her. Couldn't take her along on this ride.

"I just had a memory."

She clapped her hands. "That's great. I'm sure

being in this house will help, much more than being at Columbella."

"So why did I head there first?"

A pretty pink tide washed over her cheeks. She shifted Michael and jumped up. "I know there are dishes in the house. I'll get some bowls for the salad, anyway."

"Let's help your mom, Michael."

The boy scooted to the edge of the chair and hopped off, running ahead of Kieran to join his mother in the kitchen.

"We'll eat at the coffee table and sit cross-legged on the floor. We'll make a picnic in the house." She handed Michael a stack of bowls with a handful of paper napkins on the top, and he turned and took measured steps back to the living room.

Kieran sidled next to Devon at the sink, inhaling her floral scent. "When did you find out you were pregnant?"

The shoulder touching his pulled away. "Soon after you left on your mission. There was no way to reach you then."

She finished rinsing the forks and stuck them in the dish drainer. "I thought I'd have a surprise for you when you came home."

"Did you tell my parents? My brother?"

"No. I wanted to wait and tell them with you. When we heard, when we thought… Your parents were devastated and Colin just about broke down. I couldn't tell them about Michael then. I didn't know if it would make things better or worse for them."

"Were you alone?"

She sniffled and then grabbed a paper towel to dry the forks. "Oh, no. My mom had come in from Florida and Dylan was nearby. Do you remember my twin brother, Dylan?"

"Nope."

"Plates." Michael had returned to the kitchen, holding out his arms.

Devon dropped a hand to his head. "Tell you what, sweet pea, let's use the paper plates from Vinnie's. That will be more fun...and less work."

Michael tugged on Devon's arm and she bent over. He put his lips to her ear and cupped his hand against her face, which flushed with color.

"Kieran's my friend, sweet pea. This is his house." She handed him the forks. "Now go put these on the napkins next to the bowls."

As he scooted out of the kitchen, Kieran turned to Devon. "Is he afraid of me?"

She looked down, her long lashes shielding her eyes. "Just a little confused. I—I didn't, don't date much."

"Maybe it's too much for him, Devon. He's a very troubled boy."

"No." She smacked her fist on the counter.

"He's not a troubled boy. He's happy and curious and friendly, he's just...he's just..."

Instinct took over. He gathered Devon into his arms, stroking her silky hair, his fingers remembering the path down each strand. She trembled against his chest and he rested his cheek against her head. He'd been wanting to hold her ever since he'd spotted her walking down Coral Cove's Main Street. He curled one hand around her neck.

"Stop!" Small fists pummeled his legs.

"Michael!" Devon broke away from his embrace and grabbed Michael's shoulder. "Michael, stop."

The boy wrapped both arms around Devon's thighs, nearly knocking her over with the force of his small body.

"Apologize to Kieran."

Kieran took two steps back from Devon and his son clinging to her. His gut wrenched. "It's okay. I wasn't hurting your mom, Michael, but you're a good protector."

Devon peeled Michael from her legs and tilted his head with her finger beneath his chin. "Is that what you thought? That Kieran was hurting me?"

Michael nodded, his hands still curled into white-knuckled fists.

"Oh, no." She pulled Michael back into her arms for a hug. "Kieran would never, ever hurt me...or you. Not ever."

Kieran closed his good eye, welcoming the darkness. How could Devon be so sure of that? How could he?

DEVON BRUSHED HER fingers together and flipped the empty pizza box closed. Another half pizza remained but they'd done a fair amount of damage to that one, too. Michael had eaten more than he had in weeks. Maybe it was the sea air. Maybe it was his burst of violence against Kieran.

Her son had never before hit anyone or anything in his life. And he had to start with his own father.

And what a moment he'd picked.

Kieran had finally taken her in his arms, held her close, shown some emotion. She'd wanted to melt into him, somehow bring him back to his former self with her energy. But the wary stranger with the closed-off face remained.

Kieran tossed a piece of crust onto his paper plate. "That was the best pizza I've had since the last time I had Vinnie's. Do you want another piece, Michael, or are you as stuffed as I am?"

Michael picked up a crust from his plate and ripped it in half. Then he scrambled to his feet and scampered toward the bathroom.

Devon sighed. "Believe it or not, he seems to be getting a little better."

"I was blunt in the kitchen, Devon, but Michael needs help."

"I know. Like I said, he has his first appointment with Dr. Estrada tomorrow. The offer still stands if you want to come along."

Her cell phone buzzed and she held up one finger. "Hello?"

"Devon, it's Gary from the garage. I got your tires on, but I didn't have a window. I covered it with a piece of cardboard and I put in an order online tonight. You going to be here for a few weeks?"

Her gaze trailed to Kieran, picking up the pizza boxes and paper plates. "Yes, I'll be here for a few more weeks."

"Good. I can install it for you then. If I drive over in your car, can you give me a ride back to the shop and my car?"

"Sure. I'm at the Roarkes' house on Coral Cove Drive. You know it?"

"Yeah, across from Columbella House, right?"

"That's it. We'll be waiting for you."

Kieran strolled out of the kitchen, hands in pockets. "Is your car ready?"

"Yeah, he's bringing it over. You're going to stay here, right?"

"I need to pick up a few things I left at Columbella."

She shivered and glanced at the closed bathroom door. "Stay out of that burned room. A man died there."

"I was reading about that when you got back from talking to the cops. Apparently, Colin saved Michelle Girard from a maniac."

"Mr. Brunswick. Didn't you have him for algebra?"

He lifted a shoulder and the corner of his mouth twisted. Is that the closest he could get to a smile?

"Leave it to my brother to save the day."

"He wanted to save you, too, Kieran. He can't quite forgive himself for leaving you."

"He needs to get over it."

"Can you?"

"I don't blame Colin. I don't remember when he and the others escaped, but when the army told me about it, I never faulted the other guys."

"I didn't mean…"

Michael burst back into the room, and Devon sealed her lips. She didn't want to talk about Kieran's ordeal in front of Michael. She needed alone time with Kieran. She needed to know where he stood. Was he ready to be a father? Did he even want the job?

"Is your place close?"

"It's my mom's place. Nothing's too far apart in Coral Cove, but it's on the east side of town, past downtown."

"And the auto shop is on the way?"

"Yeah." She tilted her head. "I'm sure we'll be

fine. At least I have two new tires. I'll take care of getting a new license tomorrow."

He dug a cell phone from his pocket. "I have one of those prepaid phones. Put my number in your phone and give me a call when you get home."

Her heart fluttered. Was he making a stand? Did he care enough to want to protect them? She entered the phone number taped to the back of his phone into her cell, and a glow touched her heart as she typed his name.

Kieran Roarke was back, and even if he wasn't the same man who'd left her side and left her bed, she'd take what she could get right now.

When Gary pulled up in her car, Devon touched Kieran's forearm. "You know Gary. You might as well get started now."

Kieran nodded and flicked on the porch light before swinging open the door. Gary exited the car and nearly tripped over the curb.

"Is that Kieran Roarke?"

"Back from the dead."

"Son of a…" Gary swept the grease-stained cap from his head and charged forward, arm outstretched. "So you made it out of there. Just like in the old days on the football field. Nothing can keep you down."

The two men pumped hands, and Gary pointed to his own eye. "Did you lose an eye over there, man?"

"Not quite, but I'm not sure I'll ever have use of it again."

"What the hell. You're alive, right?"

"Yeah, I'm alive."

"Devon, good to see you, too, and this is your little guy?" Gary bent over and waved at Michael, who had shrunk behind Devon, clutching her hand.

Great. Another stranger. Like father, like son. Michael was going to have to relearn a few things, too.

"Yes, this is Michael." She knelt beside her son. "This is Gary. He fixed Mommy's car and now we're going to give him a ride back to his car."

She said an awkward goodbye to Kieran, promising to call him when she got home. After dropping off Gary, she drove back to her mother's house, checking her rearview mirror. There were a few cars on the road, probably tourists heading from dinner to the few bars in town or making their way to the coast for more action. No white vans.

Why had someone broken into her car just to get a purse? Maybe he slashed her tires after discovering how little money she had in that purse.

She turned off Main Street and cruised past a development with a big warehouse store, an office supply store and a linens store along with the requisite coffee place and a couple of fast-food joints. A pair of headlights had followed her through downtown Coral Cove and stayed with her past the stores on the right where she'd expected him to peel off.

She continued on to the next streetlight and pulled up next to a car filled with teens, the bass from the car stereo thumping so loud it reverberated in her chest. She shifted her gaze to her rearview mirror and studied the car behind her—a sedan, not a van.

Her pulse ticked faster. Was that the same sedan at the lookout? She'd been focused on the van, but maybe the occupant of the silver sedan had been the one who broke into her car.

With her heart thumping along with the bass from the hip-hop song, Devon pulled in front of the teens' car and barreled through the red light. The teenagers got a kick out of her move and honked and flashed their lights.

She careened around the next corner and then took a few side streets to backtrack to the shopping center. The box store was closed for the night but a steady stream of cars flowed through the fast-food drive-through windows, and a few caffeine junkies had parked themselves at the coffee house.

She backed into a parking slot in front of the

coffee house, her nose pointing toward the main road. She didn't know what she was looking for—plenty of light-colored sedans criss-crossed the parking lot, pulling in and out of spaces.

"Where are we going, Mommy?"

"I thought we'd stop for some ice cream. Do you want an ice-cream cone?"

The phone in her pocket buzzed and she jumped. She checked the display and seeing Kieran's name almost made her jump again until she remembered her fiancé was no ghost.

He was no fiancé, either.

"Hi, Kieran."

"Aren't you home yet?"

"N-not quite."

His voice sharpened. "What's wrong?"

"We stopped at the local Mr. Frosty for an ice-cream cone because we didn't get enough pizza."

"Is it safe?"

"There are tons of people here, or at least tons for Coral Cove."

"I still want you to call me when you get home."

"Will do."

When she ended the call, she felt Michael's eyes boring into her. She tapped the phone. "That was Kieran checking up on us. Too bad he can't join us for ice cream."

And to escort them the rest of the way home.

As she turned from the counter, two cones in her hands, she almost bumped into the teenage boy who lived next door to her mom's house.

"Sorry, Ms. Reese."

She looked past him and his two friends punching each other in the arm. All too young to drive. "Is your mom here, Casey?"

His freckled face reddened up to the roots of his hair. "No. She's going to pick me up later."

"Do you and your friends need a ride home now? Or at least when my son and I finish our ice cream?"

"Yeah, sure. We'll take a ride."

And just like that, she had her escorts home. Not that she wouldn't still be checking her rear-view mirror for silver sedans.

But why should she? If someone broke into her car, stole her driver's license and twenty bucks, and then slashed her tires, what would he still want with her now?

Maybe he'd grabbed her license so he could see her address and follow her home. Of course, he'd have a long drive up to San Francisco. Maybe that's why he was following her now—to see where she was staying locally.

She shook her head and dragged her tongue across the soft-serve vanilla ice cream. She'd been on edge ever since Mrs. Del Vecchio's murder and Michael's strange reaction to it. Now in one day, someone had broken into her car and her dead fiancé had materialized in front of her. Those two events had done nothing to calm her down.

Crunching on her cone, she wiped a napkin across Michael's mouth. She pointed to the melted ice cream dribbling down his fingers. "Are you done with that?"

He nodded and she tossed the remainder of the cone in the trash. She stepped outside into the cool night air. The boys were lounging at a table with a red-and-white-striped umbrella hanging over it.

"Are you guys ready? One of you can sit up front, and the other two can sit in the backseat with my son, Michael."

Apparently, teenage boys were not as scary as grown men since Michael didn't make a grab for her when she settled him in his car seat next to one of the boys.

She glanced around the parking lot, hoping for a glimpse of the sedan.

I hope you're watching me load all these boys in my car. I'm not alone anymore.

Pulling out of the parking lot, she switched radio stations to something the boys would appreciate and hit the road.

She wasn't alone anymore. Kieran Roarke was back in town, and that man had a protective streak a mile long. It didn't seem as if four years as a prisoner of war had done anything to weaken it.

If anything, his protectiveness had grown fiercer. *He'd* grown fiercer. Would a man like that, honed to a hard granite, take to fatherhood?

One thing she knew for sure. Once he decided to take on the job, he'd be father of the year.

Chapter Five

"We're going to pick up my friend Kieran, and he's going to come with us when we visit Dr. Elena." Devon's eyes met Michael's in the rearview mirror. "You liked Kieran, didn't you?"

"I hit him." Michael pummeled an imaginary foe with his small fists.

"I know you did." She wagged a finger at his reflection. "The only reason you didn't get in trouble for that is because you thought you were protecting me. You don't have to protect me against Kieran. He's a good guy."

"He has a pirate patch."

"That's because he hurt his eye fighting bad guys."

"Bad guys?"

Michael's face crumpled and Devon bit her lip. She'd had just about the best conversation going with Michael in weeks, and she had to bring up bad guys. Had someone from the building talked a little too loudly about Mrs. Del Vecchio's murder? Michael never used to be afraid of bad guys.

Just like his dad.

"There are no bad guys anymore."

Michael responded by gazing out the window, his eyebrows drawn over his nose.

If anyone could get to the bottom of Michael's trauma, Elena could. She wasn't sure about Elena hypnotizing Michael but if she thought it would help, Devon just might allow it. She wanted her son back, and then they could work on building a family with Kieran.

Maybe Michael's skittishness was scaring off Kieran. If she'd presented him with a well-adjusted, uncomplicated boy would Kieran accept his role of fatherhood more readily? If that were the case, she didn't want him in Michael's life. Loving a child was all about taking the good with the bad.

Nothing like bad timing.

She cruised past Columbella House and Michael jabbed the window. "Columbella."

"That's right. We'll explore the beach again down there, but you have to promise not to climb up through the sea cave."

She pulled into the Roarkes' driveway, and Kieran stepped out on the porch. Must've been waiting for them.

He slid into the seat beside her, smelling of soap

and a hint of the sea. The scent took her back to cool nights wrapped in a blanket in the sand, snuggling against Kieran's warm, smooth skin. Making plans. Laughing. Loving.

"Everything go okay last night?"

Devon blinked. "I called you when we got home. Everything was fine."

"Why'd you decide to take those teens home?"

Lifting a shoulder, she backed out of the driveway. "Saved my neighbor a drive out and she brought me some squash from her garden this morning, so it's all good."

She could feel him studying her profile. She should probably come clean about the silver sedan she thought was following her, but she'd do it away from Michael. They had a lot of catching up to do…away from Michael.

"Where's Dr. Estrada's office?"

"It's downtown. She's on staff at the University of California at San Francisco, too, but she sees clients in this office only. She does research at the university." She took the turn from the coast highway onto the street that led into town. "While she's at it, she can probably recommend a good ophthalmologist in the city."

"I'm good."

"You don't want to find out if…?"

"I'm good."

She gripped the steering wheel and gritted her teeth. "Will you talk to Elena...Dr. Estrada?"

"Maybe. I'd like to see what she has to say about Michael."

Devon pressed her lips together. That's not what she had in mind, but she let it go. This new Kieran was not a man to be pushed around. Was he ever? She'd never tried before.

She'd changed, too. She'd had a protective father, fiancé and brother. One had died. One had been presumed dead. And one had gotten consumed by his career. She'd been left with a helpless mother and a helpless infant, and she'd had to step up to the plate. She'd become the protective one.

But now was not the time to assert her new-found strength.

They rolled onto Main Street, coming alive with tourists eating late breakfasts or browsing the antique shops, and surfers heading back into town after hitting the early-morning waves.

She turned off the main drag and parallel parked into a space on the street in front of a two-story stucco building.

"Dr. Estrada's office is upstairs. I'll stay with you for a little while, Michael, and then you can play with Dr. Estrada by yourself."

Michael clutched her hand as they walked up the steps, Kieran trailing behind them. She had faith Elena could break through Michael's barrier and ease his fears. Then Kieran could really get to know his son.

Elena shared the floor with a dentist, a financial adviser, a Realtor and an empty office. Kieran opened the outer door of Elena's office and Devon ducked under his arm, pulling Michael with her. Elena had left the door to her inner office ajar. She was a one-woman operation with a light indicator in the reception area instead of a receptionist.

Devon tapped on the door. "Hello?"

"Hello, be right out."

Devon stepped back from the door, and a few seconds later Elena bounded into the outer office, running a hand through her salt and pepper curls.

She enfolded Devon in a warm hug. "It's so good to see you, Devon. How's the nursing going?"

"It's going great. I work with a fantastic group of doctors, and there's nothing more satisfying than bringing babies into the world."

"And now you have your own baby."

Michael stared at Elena with his wide, brown eyes, and a lump formed in Devon's throat. Normally, he'd angrily assert that he was not a baby. Now…the stare. He seemed fixated on Elena's hair.

"Michael, this is Dr. Elena Estrada. She's going to talk to you just like Dr. Mowry did at home."

Elena knelt in front of Michael and took his hand to shake it. "Very nice to meet you, Michael. You can call me Dr. Elena, and you can talk to me about anything in the world."

Michael shook her hand, his gaze floating to her head.

"Do you like my hair?" Elena shook her curls.

"Your hair is gray."

Elena laughed. "Yes, it is. Is your grandmother's hair gray? I know your grandmother."

He shook his head. "My grandma's hair isn't gray."

Devon snorted. "Yes, it is, but she makes sure it stays blond through artificial means."

"Who has gray hair like mine, Michael?"

Michael dropped her hand and nestled close to Devon.

He hadn't mentioned Mrs. Del Vecchio since the murder. He'd called her Granny Del at her suggestion. Maybe he'd tell Elena all about Granny Del and her gray hair. It was the first time he'd even come close to referring to her.

"Elena, this is Kieran Roarke. Kieran, Dr. Estrada." Elena already knew Kieran was Michael's father, and Devon had already told Elena in advance that Michael wasn't in on the secret.

As they shook hands, Elena's thin brows rose. "I know all about Mr. Roarke. It's good to have you home, Kieran. Gary from the garage has already told half the town of your return." She pushed open the door to her inner sanctum. "Shall we get started? Your mom and…Kieran can join us first, Michael, and then if you're okay with it, just you and I will have a chat."

They all squeezed into her small office, Devon and Michael claiming the comfy, floral sofa while Kieran perched on the edge of a chair across from them. Elena settled into a deep chair, cradling a steaming mug.

"We're here to talk, Michael. You can tell me anything, and it's private. We're also going to play some games. How does that sound?"

He nodded.

Elena looked at Devon. "Mom, do you have any questions?"

"Do you think you might use hypnosis?"

"I don't think so. Michael probably just needs to process some feelings he has about death and dying…and abandonment." She shifted a glance toward Kieran.

Was that her subtle hint that she and Kieran needed to tell Michael he had a father? As Michael began to notice all the dads at the hospital day care, Devon had answered questions about his own father with vague murmurings about him being away. She'd probably done a poor job of it.

"Michael, do you want to check out the toy chest?" Elena pointed to a wooden chest in the corner, painted with brightly colored suns and flowers.

Michael shimmied off the couch and trotted toward the toy chest. He yanked it open and pulled out a squirt gun and a G.I. Joe action figure and settled cross-legged on the floor.

Elena jerked her thumb toward the door.

Devon clasped her hands between her knees. "Michael, Kieran and I are going to leave now. Is that okay? We'll be right across the street."

Michael looked up, his gaze darting toward Elena. Licking his lips, he put up his hand in a tentative wave.

Devon blew him a kiss from trembling lips.

When they left the office and Kieran shut the outer door behind them, Devon leaned against it and closed her eyes.

Kieran's hand dropped to her shoulder. "Are you okay?"

"It's just so hard to watch." She rubbed her nose with the back of her hand. "Michael has changed so much. He used to be so bubbly and friendly, so talkative and alive."

"Like you."

"Oh, I don't think I'm like that…anymore."

"That's how I remembered you—in my dreams."

She opened her mouth, but he grabbed her hand. "Let's get some lunch and talk."

Butterflies circled inside her belly. Was she

ready for this? After she'd blurted out the truth about Michael's paternity, she and Kieran hadn't had any time alone to discuss anything. Was she ready to bare her soul?

Was he?

Kieran dropped her hand when they hit the street. When Devon needed comforting, he could use that as an excuse to touch her, to be close to her. But he didn't want to make a habit of it. It would set them both up for heartache if he gave in to his urges.

He meandered down the sidewalk and his steps landed him in front of a large, plate-glass window with a sloppy burger and a mug of beer painted on the front. He looked up at the sign hanging over the door announcing Burgers and Brews.

Devon, lost in thought, stumbled against him and looked up at the gaily painted sign. "Your friend, Bryan Sotelo, owns this place. Are you sure you want to venture inside?"

"If Michael can talk to a stranger, so can I."

"Bryan's not exactly a stranger, which makes it harder for you."

He wedged a shoulder against the door. "I came back to Coral Cove to learn about my life. Skulking around like the Phantom of the Opera isn't going to help."

He pushed open the door, and gestured her to enter first...not that he was holding back or anything. The breakfast crowd had thinned out, and the lunch crowd hadn't hit full-force yet.

A guy with long hair and a tattoo snaking down his arm looked up from the long bar and smacked his palms on the gleaming surface. "Kieran Roarke. I heard a rumor you were alive."

The man vaulted over the bar and crushed Kieran in a bear hug. Kieran returned the hug with one arm, raising an eyebrow at Devon. If he had any question about whether or not he was the hugging type, this display just answered it— he wasn't.

"Man, you just missed Colin, but he knows, right?"

Kieran disentangled himself from the guy who had to be Bryan and stepped back. "No, Colin doesn't know. Army didn't want to notify anyone right away."

"Say no more." Bryan held up his hands. "You guys were into some deep undercover stuff. What happened to your eye?"

"Damaged."

"Won't stop you from hitting the waves, right, bro?"

"Probably not."

"Bryan." Devon tapped Bryan's muscled biceps. "I hate to break up this homecoming, but Kieran and I have a lot to talk about."

"I'm sure you do." He slapped Kieran on the

back. "Let's catch up later, dude. Do you two want something to drink?"

"I'll have a diet soda." Devon pointed to a table in the corner. "Can we grab that table?"

"Sure. Something to drink, Kieran? I've got some great local brews on tap."

"Little early for a beer, Bryan. I'll take an iced tea."

Devon sprinted for the table like she had a lot on her mind. He couldn't blame her. She'd waited almost five years to tell him about Michael, and he couldn't wait to hear about his son. Maybe if he knew more about him, he could figure out why the death of a friendly neighbor had spooked him so much.

He took a seat across from Devon, and his gaze lingered on her bright hair and rosy complexion. He felt as if he had to drink her in to sustain him for the next time they were apart.

Because he couldn't stay with her. He wanted to work out some way he could visit Michael, but he didn't want to be alone with the boy. He could never have him spend the night.

Bryan dropped off their drinks and a couple of straws. "Are you eating?"

They both said at the same time, "Nachos."

"Yeah, you two always did like to share the nachos, and we make 'em even better than in my dad's day. Extra jalapeños, right?"

When Bryan left, Devon studied Kieran as if preparing to dissect a frog in biology class. "You remembered, didn't you?"

"You're excited about nachos with extra jalapeños?"

She plunged her straw into her glass. "Don't dismiss it as trivial. Every little bit is a step forward."

Devon possessed a cheery optimism. Had it always been shored up by that layer of steel he sensed beneath the sunshine? A deadly combination—especially if he hoped to convince her that she'd be better off without him.

"Okay, what do you want to know?" She planted her elbows on the table on either side of her glass.

"I want to know all about Michael. I suppose you don't have any baby pictures of him."

"Are you kidding?" She dragged her big bag from the back of her chair and patted it. "I'm glad I didn't have this purse with me yesterday."

She pulled out some photos of a smiling, chubby baby and for the next half hour proceeded to tell Kieran all about his son.

He scooped up some salsa with the corner of a chip and paused. "He sounds like a great kid, happy, well-adjusted, so what happened? Why the trauma over the old lady's death?"

"I don't know. He called her Granny Del, and she'd bake him cookies and tell him stories. She was great with him. I don't think she'd ever had kids of her own. She was a widow, but her husband was long gone before we moved into that building."

"Does Michael have a good relationship with your mom? Maybe Granny Del was a substitute grandmother for him."

"I suppose." She dabbed her luscious lips with a napkin and Kieran pulled his gaze away. "He doesn't see my mom much. After leaning on me heavily after Dad's death, Mom packed up and moved to one of those retirement communities in Florida. We see her occasionally, but she tries to keep busy and active…to fill the emptiness from Dad's death."

"Your dad was the police chief of Coral Cove, wasn't he?"

"Yes. You see. There's another one of those trivial facts."

"I got the feeling Dr. Estrada was blaming me in part for Michael's trauma." Kieran shoved the plate toward Devon, and took a long pull from his iced tea. And would finding out he had a father like him only add to the boy's trauma? How could he possibly help Michael? That would be like the blind leading the blind—literally, in his case.

Devon shoved some chopped tomatoes around the plate with her fork. "I don't think she's blaming either one of us, but I do think she was implying that not having a father present may have contributed to Michael's feelings of loss when Mrs. Del Vecchio passed away."

"Passed away? She was murdered."

"Yeah, well, Michael doesn't know that—at least I don't think he does."

"What about the murder? Were you home when it happened?"

"Yeah, that's the creepy part." She hugged herself and hunched her shoulders as if shivering. "It happened mid-morning. I was doing laundry and I found the body."

Kieran dropped his napkin on the table. "You're kidding me."

"Nope."

"Did you hear anything? See anything?"

"I heard noise from her apartment. It must've been a thump against the wall or something since she lives right below me. That's why I decided to check up on her after I put my laundry in. While I was in the laundry room, someone slammed the door. The cops think it might've been the killer."

His heart lurched. Devon had been in danger and he hadn't been there to protect her. Hadn't been there for four long years. "My God. It's a good thing he didn't see you or vice versa."

"You're telling me. It was awful enough finding Mrs. Del Vecchio's body."

"How was she killed?"

"The guy drowned her in the kitchen sink, like

he was dunking her head in the water over and over because she had marks on her neck."

"Brutal." And he knew brutal. "Who would do an old lady like that? Did they rob her?"

"Her place was ransacked, but as far as I know, she didn't have anything worth stealing."

"Cops have any leads?"

"Not that I know of. At least they didn't while we were still there. A Detective Marquette was working the case, and I haven't heard from him since we got here."

"Wow." He tracked his fingertip through the condensation on the outside of his glass. "Maybe it was just a crime of opportunity. Her door was unlocked, and some junkie thought he could get some quick cash."

"Maybe. I just hope Elena can get through to Michael. He hasn't said anything to me about Granny Del since I told him she was dead."

"Do you think Michael is going to be more upset when he learns he has a father?" Especially a father like him.

"I don't know. He started asking questions a few years ago, and I was vague." She drew criss-cross patterns in the plate. "Maybe somehow he figured out that his father was dead, and when Granny Del died, too, he couldn't handle any more loss."

Kieran's injured eye ached and he dug the heel of his hand into his good eye as if that could stop it. He'd known coming back to this place was going to be hard, but he didn't know it would cause gut-wrenching grief…and indescribable joy.

"Are you okay?"

He dropped his hand and adjusted his patch. "It pains me sometimes, my eye."

"How much do you remember about us, Kieran? When I first saw you on the beach, you said you didn't remember me but you knew me. Then you tried to back away from that. Which is it?"

This woman with her golden hair and clear blue eyes had a core of granite. If he'd expected his angel to be soft, yielding and pliant, he'd have to adjust those expectations.

"You saved my life, Devon."

Her eyes widened. "I—I did?"

"I didn't remember a woman, Devon Reese, but I remembered an ideal, a vision of warmth and goodness and pure happiness."

A tear wobbled on the edge of her lashes and the tip of her nose reddened. "You're going to be so disappointed."

No. She was the one headed for disappointment.

He had to get off this subject of expectations and disappointments. He glanced at the clock on the wall. "Two hours is almost up. I hope she made some progress with Michael."

"And you? Will you give her a chance to help you, too?"

"Maybe."

"When are you going to tell your parents and Colin?"

"From what I gather, Colin is incommunicado. I'll notify my parents when I feel comfortable in my own skin."

As they pushed back from the table, a pretty blonde covered her mouth and squealed. "Kieran Roarke. Now I believe you're really back."

Kieran gripped the back of his chair and he murmured to Devon. "Who's that?"

She whispered back. "Britt. You dated her in high school."

Britt wasted no time in crossing the room and throwing her arms around him. He forced himself not to shrink away from the personal contact...or worse, throw Britt to the ground.

"How are you, Britt?"

"So much better now that I've seen you. I'm so happy you made it out alive."

"You and me both." He patted her shoulder awkwardly. "Devon and I have to run, but it was great seeing you. I hope we have time to catch up soon."

She wiped a tear from her cheek and nodded. "So thrilled to have you back, Kieran. I'm working at the library now. Stop by any time."

Wow, that Kieran Roarke must've been a helluva guy.

They stepped into the sunshine and Kieran blinked as Devon nudged him in the side with her elbow. "Britt was your girlfriend in high school and the head cheerleader."

"Maybe I should've acted more excited to see her."

"I think you're doing okay. People can't expect you to want a ticker-tape parade or anything."

"God, I hope not."

They strolled back to Dr. Estrada's office, and the sun warmed Kieran's shoulders. He took a deep breath of the tangy air. He'd missed that smell. It was in his blood…just like the woman next to him.

Before they hit the staircase, Devon jiggled the handle to the bathroom on the ground floor. "It's locked. I wonder if Elena has a key."

Kieran ushered her up the stairs ahead of him and watched the sway of her hips as she took each step. Every small movement of her body seemed to call out to him.

Devon slipped into the doctor's outer office and stood by the inner office door, her fingers threaded in front of her. Kieran wanted to ease her tension in some way, to comfort her, but he couldn't take his rightful place as Michael's father…not yet. He slumped in a chair and leafed through a magazine.

The door swung open, and Devon jumped back. "All done?"

Dr. Estrada smiled and patted Michael's back. "We got to know each other a little better."

"Do you want lunch, Michael?" Devon's smile was wide enough to split her face.

Michael nodded and cast a half smile at Dr. Estrada.

"Oh, Elena, do you have a key to the bathroom downstairs?"

"Yes, all the tenants do." She reached into a basket on one of the tables and pulled out a big, wooden keychain. "Just bring it back."

"Michael, do you need to use the bathroom, too?" Devon held up the key.

"Uh-huh." Michael skipped to the front door.

Was Devon trying to leave him alone with Dr. Estrada? The woman didn't surrender easily.

"We'll be right back. Maybe you and Elena can get better acquainted."

The door whispered shut behind her and Kieran stuffed his hands in the pockets of his jeans. "You know I'm Michael's father?"

"Even before you returned, Devon had told me the identity of Michael's father. Not the best timing, is it?"

"It would be difficult to break the news to a well-adjusted kid. Michael's trauma makes it harder."

"It might help Michael to gain a father right now, but let's talk about you for a minute."

"What did Devon tell you?"

"The basics—prisoner of war, physical torture, memory loss. Does that about sum it up?"

"In a nutshell."

"But there's more, isn't there? More you'd rather not tell Devon."

He shrugged off the question. More Devon didn't need to know, which meant getting out of her life. "I'd like to reclaim more of my memories before contacting my family. Being here in Coral Cove has helped."

"Have you ever been hypnotized before?"

"Not completely successfully. I was a Green Beret. We were trained to resist such tactics."

"But if you don't resist?" She spread her hands. "Who knows? Maybe if you go willingly, we can dig out more of your memories."

"I'll think about it. When is Michael's next appointment?"

"In two days." She pulled a card out of the pocket of her skirt, cupped it in her hand and wrote on the back. "I'll give Devon a call later, and tell her, and you, about Michael's progress today. I have another patient coming in, so Devon can drop the bathroom key in the basket."

"Okay, I appreciate…"

A crash from outside made them both jump.

"What was that?" Elena ran to the window and shoved aside the blinds. "Is that smoke?"

A chill raced up Kieran's spine. "Where?"

"It looks like it's coming from this building… the first floor."

Kieran charged out of the office and took the steps two at a time on his way down. He turned the corner and staggered backward, away from the black smoke billowing out of the small window of the bathroom.

The bathroom containing Devon and Michael.

Chapter Six

The bathroom exploded. Bits of tile and plaster rained on Devon's head as she hunched over Michael to protect him from the fallout. The smell of gasoline flooded her nostrils and her eyes burned.

Whimpering, Michael reached for the lock on the door. She knocked his hand away and then clutched it in remorse. "Wait."

She placed her hand against the metal door of the stall. It warmed her palm. The fire must be on the other side, leaping in anticipation.

The bathroom contained two stalls, and she and Michael were in the one farthest from the door. She dropped to her hands and knees and peeked beneath the stall. Flames licked up the walls of the bathroom, blackening the mirror.

"This way." She crawled into the next stall, dragging Michael with her.

Someone banged on the bathroom door. "Devon! Devon!"

Gasping, she dragged herself to her feet and

pressed her body against the stall door. The fire was raging outside of this stall, too. How could they get to Kieran? How could he get to them through the locked door?

"We're here, Kieran! I can't get to the door."

Gunshots rang out, and she screamed. Her throat felt raw.

Another gunshot. A thump. A whoosh of air as the door burst open.

Kieran's voice cut through her fear. "Is Michael okay?"

"He's with me."

"Good. Pick him up. Push open the stall door as hard as you can and keep moving forward. I'm here. I can get you out."

She grabbed Michael and hoisted him in her arms. He clung to her neck, eyes wide. She backed up to the toilet and coiled her muscles. She kicked out one foot and the stall door slammed outward.

Kieran appeared amid the smoke, holding his shirt or sweatshirt out to her. "Duck in here. Hurry. Don't look around."

She hunched forward, clutching Michael to her chest and burrowing into the clothing Kieran held out to them. He wrapped the material around their heads and yanked them outside.

When the sweatshirt came off her head, Devon gulped in lungfuls of air. Kieran scooped Michael from her arms and with his hand at the small of her back, propelled her forward. "Keep moving."

She stumbled alongside Kieran out to the street as sirens pierced the air. He grabbed her arm and pulled her toward a grassy strip bordering the sidewalk.

When they were clear of the building and the smoke, Devon spun around to face the scene. Two fire engines had pulled up alongside the stucco office building. Firefighters hauled equipment and hoses from the trucks as the bathroom continued to belch black smoke.

She shuddered and sank to the grass. Kieran crouched beside her, bringing Michael with him. Michael clung to Kieran's neck, his eyes squeezed shut.

"What happened in there, Devon?"

Running fingers through her sooty hair, she said, "I don't know. We were in the stall and I heard the window break. Two seconds later, an explosion rocked the bathroom. The flames took off immediately. I—I think the stalls protected us from the fire and the explosion."

"Probably." He gazed at the firefighters' activity with his dark eye narrowed to a deadly slit. "Did you see what came through the window?"

"What came through the window?" She shook her head, trying to clear the smoke from her brain. "I didn't see anything come through the window."

She pressed her hands against her bouncing knees, and Kieran ran a soothing hand down her thigh. "I think someone threw some sort of home-made bomb or explosive device through the window."

A cold terror seized every muscle in her body. Somebody had tried to kill her...and didn't care that she had her little boy with her?

Kieran massaged her shoulder. "The ambulance is here. You and Michael are getting checked out."

"I'm okay." *Except for the shockwaves reverberating through my body.* She clapped a hand over her mouth. "What about you? Did you get burned?"

"A little on my hands." He held his strong, capable and amazingly steady hands in front of him. "Let's get you two checked out, and maybe one of the firemen can tell us what they found."

She rose to her feet, holding Michael's hand, and immediately grabbed for Kieran's arm as her knees wobbled. Kieran put one arm around her and scooped up Michael with the other.

The building's tenants and occupants stood staggered on the sidewalk watching the action. Elena ran up to them.

"Oh, my God. Are you all okay? When we saw the smoke coming from below, Kieran took off like a shot. I hadn't even connected the noise and fire with the bathroom."

"We're fine, Elena. It looks like the fire didn't progress out of the bathroom, so the building's okay."

"Who cares about the building? As long as you and Michael—" she turned to Kieran "—and Kieran are okay."

"I think they're fine." Kieran pointed to the EMTs. "But they're going to get checked out."

Still carrying Michael, Kieran grabbed Devon's hand and led her to the ambulance. "These two were in the bathroom when the fire started. I pulled them out."

The EMTs went into action, checking her and Michael's vital signs. She told them about her scratchy throat and one of the EMTs sprayed a numbing agent against the back of her throat. Michael got some drops in his eyes, but they didn't seem to be any worse for wear after their close call.

What did it all mean?

Chief Evans rolled to a stop in his unmarked car and sauntered toward the first fire engine. "You boys have this under control?"

The fire captain said something to the chief and then gestured toward Devon. Great. Showtime.

Chief Evans ambled toward her, seemingly in no hurry to get to the bottom of the fire. Or the attempt on her life. "Devon Reese?"

"Yes." The EMT held up the eye drops and she shook her head.

"I'm Chief Evans."

"I know." She tipped her chin at Kieran. "And this is Kieran Roarke."

The men shook hands and Evans said, "I've heard of the Roarkes, and I just met your brother, the FBI agent."

"You weren't chief when I lived here."

Kieran's voice hovered halfway between a statement and a question, but Chief Evans had no reason to question Kieran's memory. "I was one chief after Ms. Reese's father, but his reputation lives on."

This trip down memory lane was all well and good, but the chief had a crime to solve. "You can call me Devon, or call me lucky since I was in that bathroom with my son when it blew up."

"Michael?" Kieran rubbed a black smudge on his very white face. "Do you want to stay here in the ambulance while your mother and I talk to Chief Evans and the firefighters?"

The EMT gestured to a cot in the back of the ambulance. "We want to run a few more tests on him. He looks fine, but he could've inhaled some smoke."

"I'll stay with him." Elena hopped on the back of the ambulance next to Michael, and he scooted closer to her.

Kieran purposely strode away from Michael, out of earshot.

Before Devon even got started, Chief Evans snapped his fingers. "You were robbed yesterday, weren't you?"

"Yeah, I was and I'm wondering if that has something to do with the fire in the bathroom."

He cocked his head, his brows creating a *V* over his nose. "Really? You'll be happy to hear we found your purse—no money, but the thief left your driver's license."

Maybe it *had* been a simple theft. "Do you have it with you?"

"No, it's back at the station. So what happened here today?"

"My son and I were using the restroom, just finishing up in a stall, when I heard the window smash. Almost immediately there was an explosion and a fire."

"Sounds like a Molotov cocktail to me." This time Kieran's voice held no note of uncertainty. He may have forgotten the details of his life, but his military knowledge and skills hadn't suffered.

Chief Evans twisted his head around to study Kieran. "Are you an FBI agent, too?"

"No." Kieran's hands curled into fists. "But I know a lot about explosives."

"I suppose the arson investigators can tell us more." The chief jerked his thumb at the scorched-out bathroom where the firefighters had already doused the flames in the small enclosure and were tromping through the ruins. "How'd you get out?"

"Kieran dragged us out."

"You *are* lucky."

Actually, luck had nothing to do with the rescue and Kieran had everything to do with it. "I don't feel very lucky with someone trying to kill me."

Chief Evans sucked in a breath. "Is that what you think?"

She raised her eyes to the sky. "Let's see. I'm the only one in the bathroom with my son and some lunatic throws some kind of bomb through the window. Yeah, I'd say someone's trying to kill me."

Kieran snorted, and the chief shot him a look from beneath his heavy eyebrows. "Maybe the perpetrator didn't realize you were in the bathroom, Devon. Maybe someone in the building was the target or the building itself."

"The building was a target?"

"We'll look into the owner, insurance, debts and so on. Also, the office next to the bathroom belongs to an attorney, a family-law attorney. He could've been the target of an irate spouse or parent."

She stole a look at Kieran and his unreadable expression. Even without the eye patch, she didn't think his emotions would play across his face.

Made it hard for her to read him, and she'd never had that problem before.

"I definitely think I'm the prime target here, Chief. This happens a day after someone breaks into my car and slashes my tires?"

"Someone stole your purse and vandalized your car. It's a big leap to murder." Chief Evans's jaw tightened. He seemed more interested in refuting her suspicions than investigating the crimes against her. Could she help it if her father had left a pair of big shoes to fill?

Maybe the thief had murder on his mind yesterday, too, but Kieran's presence at the beach had stopped him. She crossed her arms and dug her fingers into her flesh. And the teenagers' presence had stopped him last night.

The chief coughed and flicked a handkerchief out of his pocket. "Any reason why someone would target you for murder?"

Devon licked her lips, fingers digging deeper. "A woman was murdered in my apartment building in the city. Th-that's why I brought my son down to Coral Cove."

The chief's nostrils flared and his eyes lit up. "You witnessed the murder?"

"No."

"Then why would the killer follow you down here?" He straightened his cuffs and blew out a breath. "We've had enough murders in Coral Cove to last us the next fifty years."

"Maybe this guy doesn't realize you reached your quota."

"My men have been canvassing the area to see if anyone noticed anything. The window was on the side of the building, so he could've gotten away down that alley." He stuck out his hand. "We'll be in touch, Devon."

Both she and Kieran shook hands with him and turned away.

"By the way."

Without turning her body, she cranked her head around. "Yeah?"

"I heard your brother, Dylan, is applying for my position when I leave."

"Yes."

"I suppose the folks in town will like having a hometown boy back in the saddle."

She shrugged. "I guess."

Especially with a current chief who seemed more concerned with the city's image than protecting its citizens.

As they hurried back to Michael, Kieran leaned in, almost touching her ear with his lips. "Does he have an inferiority complex or something?"

"Sounds like it. I don't know him well. He took over as chief after my mom moved, so I've just seen him around when I've been down on visits."

"I don't like his style, but I have to admit he made a few good points." He held up his hands when she turned on him. "Let's see what he comes up with regarding ownership of the building and that attorney. Hell, it could be some angry client of Elena's."

She wiped her clammy hands on the back of her shorts. It could be. She hadn't witnessed Mrs. Del Vecchio's murder. If she had, she would've already told the police. The killer had to realize that. What could he want with her now?

Unless he figured she was too spooked to ID him. And he wanted her death as insurance she never would.

THE EMTs HAD RELEASED Michael with the caveat to watch his breathing and to bring him to the hospital at the first hint of a cough.

Not even a fast-food lunch of burgers and fries could wipe the guarded expression from Michael's eyes. They'd explained the fire as an accident, but she didn't know how much of that story Michael had swallowed. Devon hadn't gotten a chance to ask him about his session with Dr. Elena. One step forward, two steps back.

On the car ride back to her mom's house, Michael's gaze had rarely left Kieran's face. He'd probably memorized every feature and every line. Maybe he was picking up tips on keeping a poker face because now Devon couldn't read Kieran *or* Michael.

"I think a nap is in order, don't you, Michael?" She leaned into the backseat and brushed his forehead with the back of her hand. "Are you sure you're okay? How are your eyes and throat?"

"Okay."

"Good. I'm okay, too. Pretty scary stuff but we're both fine now."

When they got out of the car, Kieran took a position by the front door, crossing his arms and leaning against the doorjamb. But his casual stance didn't fool her. His hard muscles remained tense, his one visible dark eye bright and alert as if he planned to take flight at any moment.

Michael marched up to Kieran and patted him on the kneecap. Kieran stuck out his fist for a knuckle bump and Michael's small hand met his. "No problem, buddy."

Devon's brows shot up. These two had trouble communicating with her but seemed to read each other's minds. She held out her hand, wiggling her fingers. "You need that nap."

Michael grabbed her hand, and they ambled down the hallway to her brother Dylan's old room. After she tucked Michael in and left the bedroom door ajar, she returned to the living room where Kieran had taken a seat in the breakfast nook, his dark dangerousness incongruous amid her mother's cheery yellow pitcher and flowered tablecloth.

"So what was that all about?" She jerked her thumb over her shoulder at the front door. "Some secret code?"

"He was thanking me for getting you two out of that bathroom." Kieran stretched his long, denim-clad legs in front of him. "He'd been thinking about it on the ride home, sizing me up."

"I'm glad you were there, Kieran. I expected Michael to go off the deep end after the explosion and fire. He was obviously upset, but not as much as I expected." She pulled out the chair across from him and dropped into it. "I think it's because you saved us."

A muscle twitched in his lean jaw. "Bad timing."

"The explosion? When is a Molotov cocktail flying through a bathroom window *not* bad timing?"

"I meant all of this. Me. You. Michael."

Her blood ran hot in her veins, and she had to hook her feet around the legs of the chair so she wouldn't shoot out of it. "Well, I'm sorry I couldn't present you with the perfect son at the perfect time."

His tanned skin flushed a dark red, and his single eye glittered. The fingers he'd been drumming on the tabletop stilled. "Michael is perfect."

She swallowed the lump in her throat. "This reunion... It's nothing how I dreamed it would be."

"I'm sorry I couldn't present you with the perfect fiancé."

A hot tear splashed on her cheek. "You are perfect, Kieran. You're alive and that's all I ever prayed for."

"I'm not the same man who left Coral Cove over four years ago."

She grabbed a napkin from her mom's colorful ceramic napkin holder and blew her nose. "I'm not the same woman. Maybe you don't realize that because you don't remember enough about me. But believe me, I've changed. People change."

Kieran slid a finger beneath the elastic band securing the patch around his head. He peeled up the patch. "I'm damaged."

Unflinching, Devon studied his eye. She reached out and dabbed the red, puckered skin with the pad of her fingertip. Kieran's breath blew hot against her palm. The spiky, black lashes that formed a crescent high on his cheekbone stirred.

"Can you open it?"

His lid twitched, and he opened his eye, showing a sliver of black iris. "Not much."

"It's too soon to tell whether or not you'll see out of that eye again. But if you don't," she shrugged, "I can't imagine that stopping you from doing whatever it is you want to do, Kieran. Nothing ever stopped you before—not your dyslexia when you were a kid and not a two-hundred-fifty-pound linebacker. A little eye injury is not going to bring you down now."

He laughed, not the booming, infectious sound from his former life but a short, sharp staccato, as if he was unaccustomed to the practice. He slipped the patch back over his eye. "Has anything ever stopped you before? I showed you my eye to scare you off, and you take a clinical look at it and dish out the Pollyanna advice."

She slumped back in her chair. At least he'd admitted that he was trying to scare her off, but why? She'd been through nursing school and had been an RN for several years. Did he really think an inflamed eye was enough to send her running for the hills?

Did he think she'd reject him because he was blind in one eye? But she hadn't, so why push her away?

She had changed. She'd learned to tackle issues head-on, and she had no intention of shying away from this one. She straightened her spine and planted her feet flat on the floor.

"What is it, Kieran? I'm not bothered by your eye or the fact that you may permanently lose your sight. In fact, the patch... Well, it's kind of sexy."

He lifted one brow and murmured. "Pollyanna."

Grinding her heels farther into the wood floor,

she said, "I want to know. If you don't love me anymore or think you can't learn to love me again, let's have it. I can take it."

That was a total lie. If he admitted he couldn't love her, she'd fall apart...just not in front of him and not in front of Michael. She'd never fall apart in front of Michael.

Kieran's expression never changed. He shifted in his seat and opened his mouth, but whatever he'd started to say was drowned out by a wail from Michael's room.

Chapter Seven

Kieran shot to his feet, adrenaline pumping through his system full force. He recognized that sound. God, he recognized that sound.

Devon jumped up, too, her head tilted to the side. She placed a hand on his arm. "He has nightmares."

He charged past her and shoved open Michael's door. Michael screamed again, his back bolted to the headboard, his eyes staring vacantly in front of him.

Pain hammered the back of Kieran's skull. His hands clenched. He wanted to rip something apart. He wanted to smash his fist through the wall.

His son trembled on the bed, halfway between wakefulness and a sleep that clutched and dragged him back to the horrors of his nightmare.

Devon hovered behind him and Kieran dragged in a deep, steadying breath. This wasn't his nightmare. It was Michael's, and his son needed him, needed him to be calm and sure, not a raging lunatic ready to do violence.

He took a step toward the bed and whispered, "Michael."

Michael's fists bunched the bedclothes. His eyes flickered. His next scream gurgled in his throat and died with a whimper.

Kieran perched on the edge of the mattress. "It's okay, Michael. It's just a dream. Dreams can't hurt you."

Michael sucked in a breath of air and let it out with a whistle. His brown eyes darkened. His grip on the covers loosened.

"That's it. Push the dream away. Your mom's here."

"Mom?" Michael rubbed his nose and blinked his eyes.

Devon crept toward the bed as if afraid she'd break a spell. "I'm here."

Leaning forward, she kissed Michael's head. "It was just a bad dream, sweet pea. Do you remember what it was about?"

"No."

"Just scary, huh?" She pulled him from the jumbled covers and wrapped her arms around him. "If you remember what it was about, you can tell Dr. Elena. She likes to hear about dreams."

"She told me."

"Good." She ruffled his hair. "That wasn't much of a nap."

Michael's features sharpened, and Kieran understood his son didn't want to return to dreamland. Why would he want to return to a world of fears and threats and monsters?

"Why don't you bring your blanket with you, and join your mom and me in the living room? If you feel tired, you can fall asleep and we'll be right there with you."

Michael scrambled from the bed, dragging a small blanket with him, and Devon mouthed the words "thank you."

Michael curled up in a corner of the couch, facing the TV. Devon tucked the blanket around him and plumped a pillow behind his head.

"I get the hint." Devon opened a cabinet and held up a couple of DVDs. "Which one?"

Michael pointed at one with animated fish on the cover, and Devon slid it into the DVD player. She raised an eyebrow at Kieran. "Are you joining us?"

Did he have a choice? The woman was relentless. She was probably hoping Michael would conk out in minutes and she could resume her third-degree interrogation. He could withstand the Taliban, but Devon Reese was in a whole other category, even though he didn't have any better answers ready this time around.

If he told her the truth, she'd shrug it off, suggest a remedy, find the silver lining. She was good at that.

She apparently didn't have a problem with a one-eyed man. Not that he expected her to. She was still as loyal and pure as the woman of his dreams—the good dreams.

He dropped to a cushion on the couch, and she settled next to him, between him and Michael. Michael stretched out his legs across his mother's lap.

One cozy family...until the nighttime terrors.

"Hmm, I wish we had some popcorn." Devon tickled the soles of Michael's feet. His giggle turned into a cough.

"Do you want some water?" Kieran half rose from the couch.

"Yes, please."

Kieran exchanged a glance with Devon. Michael seemed to be talking more. He'd suffered two traumas today, and instead of thrusting him back into his shell, the experiences seemed to be coaxing him out.

Kieran ambled to the kitchen, in no hurry to get back to the talking and singing fish. While he poured a glass of water for Michael, the boy's cough worsened.

He returned and handed the glass to Michael once he'd settled down after another coughing fit.

"That doesn't sound good, sweet pea, and you

know what the EMTs said." Devon rubbed circles on Michael's back as he sipped the water. "Is your throat scratchy?"

"A little." He took another gulp of water and then coughed up most of it.

"Okay, that's it. I'm taking you to the hospital. We both breathed in a lot of smoke in that bathroom—icky smoke. I'm just following up on the EMTs' orders."

"I agree." Kieran held out his hand for the empty glass, and Michael's dark eyes searched his face.

"Can you come?"

"Of course I'll come." He pointed to his eye patch. "I've spent a lot of time at hospitals recently."

"Fire?"

He shrugged. "Just an accident."

By the time they got to the hospital Michael had lapsed back into silence, but Kieran had hope Dr. Elena could help him. They hadn't even gotten a chance to talk to her about the session today. Too much excitement.

After the doctor examined Michael, he gestured Devon and Kieran into the hallway. "I'd like to keep him overnight for observation. I'm going to give him an inhaler to use tonight to ease his breathing and his cough. Then I'd like to take an X-ray of his lungs."

"H-he has nightmares, Dr. Jessup. I'd rather not leave him."

"We'll keep an eye on him. You can stick around for a while if you like. The anti-inflammatory medicine I'm going to give him will make him drowsy."

They spent the next few hours in Michael's room and even shared a dinner of hospital food with him. Devon wanted to spend the night in his room, but the nurses convinced her he'd get more rest if he could drift off to sleep by himself and not try to stay awake to be with his mom.

Devon told Michael before he got his next dose of medicine that she'd be leaving him there for the night. "If you need anything or have any bad dreams, the nurses will be right here to help you. They can call me and I'll be here in a flash."

She snapped her fingers. "You forgot to bring your backpack. Where is your backpack? I haven't seen it lately."

Michael hunched his shoulders. "Lost it."

"You lost your Thomas the Tank Engine backpack? What did you have in there?"

"Nothing." Michael scrunched against the pillows and pulled the covers up to his chin.

"I'll look for it at home." Devon smoothed the sheet over Michael's body. "So are you going to be okay here?"

He nodded.

Michael's easy acceptance of his fate didn't surprise Kieran. The efficiency and routine of the hospital seemed to have had a calming effect on him...but not on his mother.

They hung around until Michael was so drowsy he couldn't keep his eyes open.

Devon fidgeted on her way to the car. "Do you think he's going to be okay?"

"He's probably fast asleep right now."

"What if he wakes up? What if he has another nightmare?"

"Does he have those nightmares every night?"

"No, maybe once a week now."

"He seemed better today, at least better than yesterday."

"He did, didn't he? Talked a little more." She pulled her phone from her pocket. "Elena called while we were in Michael's room. It's probably too late to call her back tonight, but I want to find out how the session went."

"When I was talking to her—before the explosion—she seemed to think it went great, but if there had been any huge breakthroughs, she would've told you by now."

"Speaking of breakthroughs, since we're driving past town I'm going to drop by the police station and pick up my purse and license."

"Good idea. We can see if they have any leads on the fire."

The cop at the front desk handed over Devon's purse and license, but had no information about the explosion in the bathroom. "All I know is that we didn't arrest anyone this afternoon…except a drunk driver on the coast highway."

"Well, that's something, anyway." Devon signed for her belongings. "I suppose you don't have anything on the guy who stole my purse, either."

"No. A jogger found it on the side of the road. Could've just been a passerby who saw your purse in an unattended car and took his chances."

"And broke my window and slashed my tires for the fun of it?" When the cop held up his hands, Devon broke off. "Whatever."

They turned to leave and the cop stopped them with a cleared throat. "You're Kieran Roarke, right? You're the one who broke into the bathroom and saved Ms. Reese?"

"I am."

"You didn't happen to blow through that lock with a .45, did you?"

"Yeah, I did. The gun's licensed to my father. I found it at his house."

The cop looked down and shuffled some papers on the desk. "Uh, the chief might want to talk to you about that. You need a license to carry a concealed weapon."

"He knows where I'm staying, and I'm a member of the U.S. military. I think I know how to handle a gun."

They walked into the cool, clear night and Devon stared at his profile. "You had a gun all this time?"

"I found it last night in my parents' house. Cleaned it and took it with me this morning. Good thing I did."

"Yeah, but you can't just run around carrying a gun."

"Sure I can." And he had every intention of keeping the weapon handy as long as someone might be after Devon. The army hadn't discharged him yet.

They got into Devon's car and she collapsed against the seat back. "Did that hospital food do the trick for you, or are you still hungry?"

"I'm good." Was she still trying to fatten him up?

"I'm going to call the hospital and check on Michael." She dug for her cell and placed the call. After a few minutes of conversation, she flashed him a thumbs-up sign. "Michael's still sleeping and he's not coughing."

She cranked on the engine and slipped him a sideways glance. "I suppose you want to head home?"

"No way."

"N-no way?"

"Someone threw a Molotov cocktail into a bathroom today—you were in that bathroom. We don't know yet if you were the target, but I don't want to take any chances."

Devon's face brightened, and Kieran swallowed hard. He didn't want to burst her bubble, but he had to make it clear he wanted to be her protector not her seducer. *Scratch that.* He wanted to seduce her but it wasn't going to happen.

"I have to admit, I'd feel safer with you at my mom's house, but I don't want to put you to any trouble."

"No trouble…except, can you swing by my place first so I can pick up a jacket?"

"A jacket? Are you cold?"

Not yet, but he'd be plenty cold keeping vigil out in her car. "Yeah."

Instead of taking the turnoff into town, Devon continued driving along the coast highway until she took the exit for Coral Cove Drive. She pulled up to the curb and cut the engine. "I'll wait here."

He reached across her body and pushed open her door. "Humor me."

She sighed, but wasted no time scrambling from the car. He felt for the house key in the pocket of his jeans and turned to ask her inside. He didn't feel comfortable with her waiting on his porch. He didn't want her out of his sight, as limited as that sight was.

A light across the street caught his attention, and he gazed over Devon's left shoulder, squinting. Was his good eye playing tricks on him?

"What's wrong?"

"I saw a light at Columbella House."

DEVON WHIPPED AROUND to face the street. "That's impossible. The electricity's off, right?"

"It was yesterday, even when I went back inside to collect my stuff."

"So you think someone's over there with a flashlight or, God forbid, a candle? The cop who came to my aid yesterday said his girlfriend had been seeing lights here, but I figured she'd seen your activity."

"There's one way to find out."

She grabbed his arm as he charged down the steps of the porch. "You're going over there?"

"What if it has something to do with the explosion in the bathroom? The slashed tires? What if someone is watching you? Following you?"

His words caused a rash of goose bumps to spread across her skin. "You're not leaving me here."

"Didn't plan on it." He grabbed her hand, and together they crossed the street to Columbella House, which showed a dark, deserted front to the casual passerby.

"How long were you staying here?"

"About a week—and I had the place to myself."

"Maybe someone took up residency when you vacated."

He pushed through the side gate and ushered her to the path that ran along the house. She pointed to the sky. "The moon is giving us plenty of light out here, but what do we do once we're inside?"

"I left candles and matches in the kitchen."

She shivered. "Just what this place needs...another fire."

When they reached a side door, Kieran pulled back the piece of plywood covering the window and reached inside to unlock the door. He swung it open and stepped into the darkness first. "Wait."

A few seconds later, the flare of a match and the scent of sulfur. Then Kieran stepped toward her, the candle's flame illuminating the sharp planes of his face. He looked more like a pirate than ever in the candlelight.

"Be careful on this floor. Some of the tile is cracked."

"Be careful with that candle."

"I'll lead the way. Hold on to my belt loop or something." He whispered, and the words made the hair on the back of her neck stand up, even though she knew he was one of the good guys.

Curling her fingers through his belt loop, she shuffled behind him, trusting him to guide her. Just like old times. They turned a corner into the sitting room, where furniture hunched beneath draped white covers looked like squat little ghosts that couldn't even muster a *boo*.

Her nostrils twitched at the smell of fire still strong in this area of the house. "Y-you saw the light in the library?"

"In the window at the side of the house. That's the library, right?"

"Through those doors." She pointed to the double doors standing open in invitation. "But we weren't exactly quiet when we broke in here."

"Maybe he's still hiding in the library, light extinguished, waiting."

She yanked on his jeans. "That doesn't make me want to go snooping around the library."

He turned, holding the candle up to her face, casting his own in shadow. With her fingers still hooked in his belt loop at the back of his jeans, Devon's arm wrapped around his waist. She left it there.

"You're not afraid of Columbella House, are you?"

"No." How could she be afraid of a place that held the memories of their love? Especially since that's all they had left.

Cupping the candle with his hand, he took a step closer, his warm breath caressing her ear. "When I got to Coral Cove, the house drew me."

She closed her eyes. His familiar masculine

scent overpowered her senses. Her breath came out in shallow spurts and she parted her lips to take in more air. Her arm, draped around his waist, sagged to his hip, and his jeans chafed her inner wrist.

"This house…" A scuttling sound propelled her against his chest and he pulled her snug against his body with one arm. His heart thudded against the palm of her hand as they stood frozen, their feet rooted to the hardwood floor.

After a few seconds that seemed like minutes, Kieran shifted his body away from hers. "Do you still want to investigate?"

Tilting her head back, she gazed into his eye, the darkness of the house rendering it black to match the patch, the dance of the flame adding sparks of light. "Do you still have that gun?"

"You didn't feel it?" He patted the pocket of his sweatshirt.

Her cheeks warmed. She didn't want to get into what she'd felt when he pulled her into his arms. "If you still have the gun, I still want to investigate."

He turned from her, and she grabbed the back of his jacket. He weaved through the furniture in the sitting room and passed through the double doors that led to the library. The smell of smoke permeated everything in this room. A gaping hole scarred one wall of the library where firefighters had barreled through the panel to the secret room to put out the flames that had threatened to devour it.

Kieran swept the beam of his flashlight across the library and its covered furniture. Where they walked, dust swirled in the shaft of light. He directed the flashlight at the floor.

"Footprints."

She studied the pool of light on the floor, which illuminated men's footprints in the dust and ash. "Could be anyone's. Could even be yours from before."

"I don't think so." He placed his running shoe over the outline, his foot exceeding the imprint.

She took a tentative step forward, poking her head into the gash in the wall. The firefighters, or someone, had removed the big four-poster bed that used to dominate the room. Larry Brunswick had died on that bed, thrown himself onto it as if diving into a funeral pyre.

Kieran's hand trailed up her arm. "I remember this room."

"From before?"

"From before. With you."

The fingertips brushing her arm caused her insides to quiver and she sucked in a breath. "We spent time here."

"We didn't fear the ghosts?"

Her tremulous lips managed a smile. "We were willing to brave anything for a few moments of privacy."

"The house drew you, too, didn't it? I knew you'd come here eventually."

She tilted her head. "I thought you didn't remember me."

"I saw you when you got here, Devon, you and Michael. Maybe even then I realized he was mine. I watched you. I waited."

She rubbed her arms. Seems a lot of people had been watching her lately—some with good intentions and some with bad. "Why didn't you talk to me?"

He shook his head. "And say what? I don't know who you are, but I feel you inside me. I don't know your name, but you kept me alive for four long years in a stinking hovel."

"And if we hadn't bumped into each other on the beach?" She pressed her hand against his chest, over his heart where its pounding reverberated against her palm.

"I don't know. Maybe I would've taken it as a sign to move on."

She bunched her fingers into his shirt. "You were willing to leave my life up to fate? Michael's life?"

"It might've been better." He gripped her hand,

squeezing the blood out of it. "How do I know all this danger surrounding you isn't coming from me?"

"What?"

"What if the government wants me to come in? What if my captors have come after me?"

Her jaw dropped. He couldn't really believe that, could he? Had his years in captivity made him paranoid? Delusional?

She yanked her hand from his strong grasp. "I don't believe that for a minute. If the army wanted you in, they'd come and talk to you, not try to kill your fiancée...your ex-fiancée."

He plowed a hand through his black hair, the ends gleaming in the candlelight. "I don't know, Devon. I feel like I'm toxic. Wherever I go, evil follows."

Tears flooded her eyes. "That's not true, Kieran. When I saw you, I knew all my prayers had been answered. You're alive, even though you don't belong to me anymore. And Michael has a father."

He brushed the pad of his thumb across her lips, and then cupped her jaw with his rough hand. "I want to be a father to Michael, but..."

"Shh." She put a finger to her lips. "I heard that noise again."

Kieran turned and took several more steps into the burned-out room. "I think it's a rat or something."

"Ugh." She followed him into the center of the room. "I can't believe most of the furniture survived the blaze."

She didn't want to hear Kieran's objections to being Michael's father. Michael needed a dad, now more than ever. She kicked a heavy dresser with the toe of her shoe. The finish had been destroyed by the flame retardant the firefighters had used to put out the fire.

"Mia St. Regis needs to come back and make some sense of this place." She yanked open the top drawer of the dresser and it came apart in her hand. "Oops."

"Is it broken?" He'd come up behind her and placed one hand on her shoulder, balancing the flashlight on top of the dresser.

She looked into the wavy mirror at their reflections. They looked like something out of a funhouse—distorted, hazy, disjointed. She wanted the old Kieran and Devon back—whole, undamaged, in love.

His touch turned into a caress and he bent his head and pressed his lips against her temple.

A scuttling sound drove her back against his chest, and he laughed. "Maybe a family of mice has taken up residence in this dresser."

She held up the larger piece of the dresser drawer by its handle. "And maybe I just destroyed their home."

The rest of the drawer broke off and dropped to the floor with a thud. Kieran crouched, his head cocked to one side. "There's a false bottom in this drawer."

Devon's heart pumped faster. "Do you remember how we used to search around this house for more secret passageways and cubbies?"

"I remember this room...and you." He rapped his knuckles against the bottom of the drawer. "Do you hear that?"

All she could hear was the blood pounding in her ears. Why couldn't he just take her in his arms and kiss her...on the lips this time...hard?

"Help me." His long fingers traced around the edges of the inside of the drawer.

Devon added her hands to his, her fingers pressing, exploring. She'd rather be exploring his body.

She felt a spring and the back of the drawer popped forward. "Got it!"

She reached forward, but he cinched her wrist. "Better make sure there are no rats in there."

"Don't try to scare me." She slapped his hand away.

She inched her hand into the cavity of the drawer, her fingertips skimming the leather edge of a book. "I think it's a book or something."

She gripped the book and pulled it out of the secret compartment. Holding it up, she said, "Look."

Kieran rubbed the sleeve of his jacket against

the red, leather-bound book, which had a small lock holding the front and back covers together. "Looks like a diary."

"Oh, maybe it belongs to some long-lost St. Regis relative. Should we snoop and break the little lock?"

"We broke into the house. What's a diary?"

Kieran tucked the book under his arm and pulled Devon back into the library. He raised the candle to peer at the lock.

Instinct drew Devon's gaze to the window.

Kieran jerked his head up. "What is it?"

"I thought I saw…"

A flash of light and a crack at the window interrupted her words. And then she had no breath to speak at all because Kieran had tackled her to the floor.

Chapter Eight

Kieran pinned Devon to the floor with the full length of his body. With his chest sealed against hers, he couldn't tell where his galloping heart left off and hers began. His breath came out in harsh gasps, stirring the strands of hair that fell across her face. "Stay down."

He grappled for the cell phone in his pocket, while he tried to scoot Devon behind the sheet-covered desk. He only succeeded in grinding his pelvis against hers. Two minutes ago that action would've driven him crazy with need. Now it caused a rush of adrenaline to flood his system, and he half picked her up from his position on top of her to hoist the two of them behind the desk with a thump against the hard floor.

After choking and making several strangled sounds, Devon forced a few words out. "What was that?"

"A gunshot."

Her body jerked beneath his, allowing him to

slip the phone from his pocket. He called 911. Should have it on speed dial by now.

"We're at Columbella House and someone shot at us through the window."

Devon's body twitched again as if he'd just reminded her why they were in their current position.

Kieran finished his conversation with the 911 operator and smoothed his hand over Devon's golden hair, like a beacon of light in the darkness. "It's okay. The guy's not going to stick around for a second shot."

"You can't tell me that's the U.S. government trying to get you to come in."

The strands of her hair got caught on his calloused palms and all he wanted to do was kiss the worry from her pursed lips.

"If you are the target, Devon, why?"

"I have no idea. The only thing I can think of is Mrs. Del Vecchio's murder, but I didn't see anything. Why would they believe I saw something? The killer shut that laundry room door on me, and my back was to the door."

"Was Mrs. Del Vecchio still alive when you found her? Did she tell you anything before she died?"

"She was dead. Why would her killer believe otherwise?"

"Did the newspaper reports of the murder identify you?"

Her eyes wide, she nodded.

"He knows you found the body. Maybe he's afraid he left a clue. Maybe he's afraid Granny Del whispered his name to you with her dying breath."

"Any clue would be for the police to find. I wouldn't know a clue if it smacked me on the forehead. And I'm sure he knew he'd finished off Mrs. Del Vecchio."

The sounds of sirens reached them as they huddled beneath the desk. Kieran had pulled the sheet around them for added security. Not that he believed for one minute the shooter would come after them in the house.

Two attempts on Devon's life in one day.

Maybe fate *had* drawn him to this house for a purpose.

An hour later, after the cops had canvassed the area, retrieved the bullet embedded in a bookshelf, and questioned them, Kieran took Devon's hand while they stood on the sidewalk in front of his parents' house.

"This is why I'm not leaving you on your own tonight."

She glanced over her shoulder at the cop car parked at the curb. "Do you think he followed us here or was waiting for us?"

"I've been keeping an eye on the rearview mirror in the car. I'd know if someone were tailing us."

"Do you remember what the man looked like yesterday at the beach? Maybe it was him. He broke into my car. Maybe he was trying to get my address here. Then he tried to follow me to my place that night."

"Whoa." Kieran held up his hands. "What do you mean he tried to follow you last night? You told me you stopped for ice cream."

"We stopped for ice cream so I could lose a light-colored sedan that looked suspiciously like the one parked at the beach yesterday."

White-hot anger surged through his body, and his eye throbbed. If he ever caught the person threatening Devon, he'd kill him.

"Are you mad that I didn't tell you?" She touched his arm.

He squeezed his eye shut. "No. I'm mad that I wasn't there. I'm mad that I wasn't there for Michael. I'm mad that I wasn't there for you when he was born."

"You couldn't help it." She tilted her chin at the cop waiting on the street. "He's waiting to follow me home. Are you sure you need that heavy jacket? It's still mild out."

It wouldn't be mild later tonight in her car. "Yeah. Get behind the wheel. I'll be right out."

He ran inside the house, snagged his jacket from a hanger in the closet and returned to Devon's car. As she peeled away from the curb, the patrol car lined up behind her.

They reached her mother's house, and the cop approached them when they got out of the car. "Just got off the radio with the station, Ms. Reese. Chief Evans would like you both to come in tomorrow."

"We'll be there, officer." Kieran stuck out his hand. "Thanks for your help. I can take it from here."

Devon walked ahead of him up to the lighted porch and patted her bag. "At least no calls from the hospital. Michael must be doing okay."

"We'll be there first thing in the morning to get him, or maybe we should wait until our talk with the chief. I don't think Michael needs to see any more policemen."

"I agree." She yawned. "Well, come on in. I—I can get you settled…in the spare room."

She dropped her gaze to the porch, and Kieran took a step back. "I'm staying out here tonight, Devon."

Grabbing the porch railing as if to steady herself, she said, "What?"

"If someone's lurking around, following you, I want to be where I can watch the house."

"That's crazy, Kieran. You need a bed and a good night's sleep."

"That's not going to happen if I'm worried about what's going on outside." He held out his hand. "Give me the keys to your car. I can get comfortable."

"So that's why you wanted your jacket. You couldn't ask for a blanket?"

"Good idea. Can I have a blanket, too?"

She dropped the keys in his hand and pushed through the front door. He wedged his foot in the doorjamb, propping open the screen door. She returned and shoved a blanket into his arms.

"This is no way for you to heal."

"Keeping you safe comes first. I can heal later."

He pivoted on the bottom step and made a beeline for her car in the driveway.

"Hey."

He turned halfway. She was not talking him out of this. "Yeah?"

"You have the keys if you change your mind."

"Get some sleep."

"I'd recommend the same for you, but I don't think it's happening."

He waved. "I'll manage."

He watched the lights go off in the house, then shoved the seat back and pulled the blanket around his shoulders.

He'd manage a lot better out here on his own

instead of in that house with that woman in the next room. The next bed.

Compared to that, watching the house from a cramped car for a killer was gonna be a breeze.

YELLOW STREAKED ACROSS the sky like a runny egg yolk, and Kieran's stomach growled as he drank in the sight of the breaking dawn. His vigil over, he stretched his legs as far as the car would allow and cranked his head from side to side. He needed food. He didn't need sleep.

He'd grown accustomed to wakeful nights, watchful nights looking for a means to escape. Looking for an opportunity to take revenge.

He avoided sleep. Sleep meant weakness, a loss of control.

The porch light died and a glow appeared at the front window. Devon rose early…unless she'd gotten a phone call from the hospital.

His gut twisted in unaccustomed anxiety—the curse of being a parent.

He couldn't believe he was a father. He needed help, therapy, before he could ever take on the role. He'd have to suck it up and give it a go with Elena Estrada. Michael deserved that. He deserved a whole father, not a fractured mess of a man.

The front door swung open, and Devon charged down the steps, her pink terry cloth robe flying out behind her along with her tousled blond hair—like some kind of good witch from the West Coast.

He barely had time to unlock the car before she'd grabbed the handle and yanked open the door.

"Are you done out here?" She crossed her arms, yanking the robe closed at the same time. "I would've been just as safe with you indoors, in a bed, with your gun by your side."

"But you were safer with me out here, watching the house and occasionally checking the perimeter."

Her mouth dropped open and her blue eyes widened in that adorable way she had of feigning outrage.

"Do you mean to tell me you didn't even sleep? You've been awake all night?"

He shrugged off the blanket and lifted his father's .45 from the console. "Now what would've been the point if I were sleeping?"

Sputtering, she yanked the blanket from his lap. "Get inside right now and have some breakfast and about a gallon of coffee…unless you want to take a nap."

"I don't need a nap." He swung one leg out of the car and planted his foot on her driveway next to pink polished toes. "But I will have that breakfast and gallon of coffee."

Devon whipped up a mean breakfast of bacon

and eggs. While she poured him a second cup of coffee, he asked, "Did you call the hospital yet this morning to check up on Michael?"

Her hand jerked and coffee splashed onto the saucer. "I did call. Everything's fine, his lungs look good and we can pick him up at ten o'clock after we talk to Chief Evans. I'm sorry I didn't mention it before. I'm not used to sharing Michael info with anyone."

Kieran stared into the dark brown liquid swirling in his cup. Was she telling him to back off? Did the thought of a co-parent for Michael make her skittish?

"I don't plan to be any kind of replacement for you in Michael's life, Devon. Is that why you decided not to tell my parents and Colin about him?"

She turned away and her hair swept across her face, hiding it from his scrutiny. "I told you. I thought the news of Michael would cause them even more grief. I wasn't sure your mom could handle any more."

"I get it. I'm glad Michael's okay." He blew on the coffee and then slurped the warm, rich brew onto his tongue. "I'll wait while you get ready to go, and then you can take me back to my parents' place so I can get a quick shower and change of clothes."

"Do you plan to sleep in the car in front of

the house until the police catch the maniac who's stalking me?"

"I plan to install motion-sensor spotlights around the house. It might upset some of your mom's neighbors, but something like that will spook a prowler."

"I'm still not sure he knows where I'm staying."

"Maybe not, but he'll find out."

She dropped the dishes in the sink and turned, gripping the counter behind her. "Then we'd better find him first."

While the shower ran, Kieran washed the breakfast dishes in the sink. The lights and maybe even a camera would help keep Devon and Michael safe, but they couldn't replace hands-on protection, especially the kind he could offer. He'd have to sleep in the house with them, or at least stay here at night. He couldn't sleep with them nearby. He couldn't subject them to his version of a night in dreamland.

Of course, if he made love to Devon all night long, neither one of them would have to sleep. The sound of the shower taunted him. He could picture the warm spray hitting Devon's naked body. The rivulets of water coursing over her smooth curves.

Drops of water splashed onto the floor, and he cursed. He'd let the soapy water fill the sink and it had crested over the lip.

So much for not needing sleep.

DEVON SETTLED ON the Roarkes' comfy couch by the window so she could keep one eye on Columbella House across the street. She'd always loved that house, but now? Even its interesting history couldn't wipe that gunshot from her mind.

She gasped. The diary. What had Kieran done with the diary when the shooting started?

He poked his head around the corner of the hallway, clutching a new set of clothes to his chest. "I'm going to hit the shower."

She opened her mouth to ask about the diary, but he'd already disappeared.

Of course, whatever they found had to be turned over to Mia, but they could sneak a peek first. Mia wouldn't mind. She'd divorced herself from Columbella House and all things St. Regis when she'd taken off in a huff after her twin, Marissa, had run off with Mia's fiancé.

At least *she'd* never had to worry about her twin, Dylan, stealing her man.

The shower blasted to life in the other room, and Devon closed her eyes. She thought she'd had Kieran last night. He'd be sleeping in the same house in the room next to hers with Michael safely at the hospital. What better scene for seduction?

Then he'd headed for the car.

She appreciated his commitment to keeping her safe, but really? He couldn't have done that inside? In her bed?

She shook her head. He'd become a complex man. Sometimes he looked at her as if he wanted to devour her, and other times he couldn't push her away fast enough.

He wore his secretiveness as a shield. He didn't have to protect her from what he'd gone through in Afghanistan. She wanted to know. To know his recent trials would be to know him...this new Kieran. She felt just as lost as he did, and she didn't even have memory loss.

The shower stopped and she closed her eyes to picture Kieran's body—lean, muscled and hard. What other scars did he bear from his captivity? He had plenty that weren't visible—and those would be the hardest to heal.

Several minutes later, a fully-clothed Kieran rounded the corner, sluicing a hand through his wet hair. "I think I need a haircut. I'm pretty sure I didn't have it this long as a Green Beret."

"It suits you." At least it suited the new Kieran, the mysterious, closed-off one.

"Are you ready?" He swept some change from the counter and shoved it into the pocket of a pair of cami cargo shorts. "Sorry you have to drive all the time. I guess I need to look into what it takes to get a driver's license when you have one functioning eye."

"I guess you need to look into a lot of things." She ignored his dark, piercing gaze and grabbed her purse. "The police station first and then Michael. What do you suppose Chief Evans wants to question us about?"

"Probably wants to find out why you have a target on your back and why you've led a killer to his cozy little town."

"That makes three of us."

Fifteen minutes later Devon pulled into a parking space at the police station. As Kieran opened the door to the station for her, she blinked back tears.

This building had been like a second home to her and Dylan when her dad was chief. It had a different vibe without him. Maybe if Dylan got the job of Coral Cove Police Chief, the atmosphere would change.

She waved at the officer manning the front desk. "Hey, Clark, we're here to see Chief Evans."

"I know that. Are you okay? Most people come to Coral Cove to get away from it all. You seemed to have brought it with you."

She snorted. "Is that what the chief's worried about? He's winding down his illustrious, if short, career with a serial killer and now a crazy bomb-throwing stalker. He didn't catch the former. Is he concerned he won't catch the latter?"

Clark reddened up to the roots of his hair. "I'm keeping my mouth shut. What happened to you, Devon? You used to be so sweet."

She slid a glance toward Kieran, pretending to study flyers on the bulletin board, and she put her finger to her lips.

"Devon, Roarke, glad you could make it." Chief Evans strode from the lunchroom in the back of the station.

Devon bit her lip, hoping he hadn't heard her. She wanted to carry her tough-girl image only so far. "I'll tell you as much as I know, Chief, but I'm afraid I'm in the dark."

"Anything might help, Devon." Tyler Davis, the mayor of Coral Cove, moseyed from the lunchroom in Chief Evans's wake.

"Oh, hi, Tyler. Are you in on this, too?"

"Anything that threatens the serenity of Coral Cove is my business." Tyler turned to Kieran. "I heard you were back in town, Roarke. Coral Cove should hold a parade in your honor."

Kieran held up his hands. "I'm good."

Tyler brushed his hands together. "Well, then, shall we get started?"

"We?"

The chief grunted. "I invited the mayor to this meeting, too. We have a lot of tourists in town at the moment. Exploding bathrooms are in nobody's best interests."

"Especially when you're in one. Lead the way." Devon spread her arms. She had a feeling the chief and the mayor were none too happy to see her return. One menace to the serenity of Coral Cove had just been vanquished. Would it take another Roarke to vanquish this one?

As Chief Evans and Tyler returned to the back of the station, Devon hooked her arm in Kieran's and stood on tiptoe to whisper in his ear. "Do you remember Tyler Davis?"

"No. Should I?"

"I'll tell you later." She rolled her eyes.

The chief led them to an interrogation room where he crossed his arms and wedged a shoulder against the wall. Mayor Davis took a seat at the table, and Devon and Kieran sat across from him.

The chief cleared his throat. "Why don't you tell us about this murder you witnessed in the city?"

"I already told you. I didn't witness the murder."

"You found the body."

"Yes, but I didn't see anything or anyone."

"Maybe the killer thinks you did."

Kieran placed his hands flat on the table and hunched his shoulders. "That's what I'm beginning to think, especially after last night."

"If I'd seen something, I would've told the police. Why can't the killer figure that out? He'd know if the detectives were already following up on any leads. I didn't give them any leads."

Tyler tapped the table with the eraser side of a pencil bearing teeth marks. "Maybe the killer thinks you're too scared to talk."

"Oh, and throwing homemade bombs at me and shooting at me are going to make me feel better?"

They spent several more minutes debating the plausibility of Mrs. Del Vecchio's killer coming after Devon until the chief pushed off the wall and took a seat at the table.

"I took the liberty of contacting the detective on the case, Detective Marquette. He's heading down here to talk with you again, Devon."

"Thanks…I think. I already told him everything about that day."

"And what about you, Roarke?" The chief studied his own entwined fingers. "You were with Devon both times. Can this have anything to do with your mission in Afghanistan and subsequent imprisonment?"

"I don't know." A muscle twitched in Kieran's jaw.

Tyler blinked rapidly. "Do you really think your captors would come after you here?"

Kieran pinned Tyler with one dark eye. "If that particular terrorist group thought I had some information, it's not completely out of the realm. But my captors? Impossible."

"Why is that?" The chief scribbled something on a pad of paper he'd flipped out of his pocket.

"They're all dead."

Devon's heart jumped. Is that how Kieran had escaped? She held her breath. She didn't want

Mayor Davis or Chief Evans to ask him to clarify. Kieran didn't want to talk about his escape.

Tyler sucked in a noisy breath, and the chief studied Kieran for a moment and then shrugged.

"I still think the most likely scenario is that the old lady's killer thinks you know something, Devon. And he wants to shut you up before you can reveal it to the SFPD."

Devon clamped her hands on her bouncing knees. "When did Detective Marquette say he was coming down?"

"I think he's heading down already, but he'll call you." The chief pushed back from the table and brushed his hands together. "Maybe once he talks to you, you should leave town."

"I think that's a good idea." Tyler slapped the table and then flushed under Kieran's glittering stare. "I—I mean to keep safe."

"I can't go back to my apartment in San Francisco. That would be even more dangerous. I'm here because I can stay in my mom's house for free. I can't afford to run all over the country to keep one step ahead of a killer."

"I'll keep Devon safe." Kieran scraped his chair back on the wood floor. "You just do your police work."

They were both silent on the drive to the hospital. Devon glanced at him sideways through her lashes a few times. She wanted to ask him about his escape, but she didn't think he'd tell her.

"We don't need to tell Michael about the shooting at the house."

He turned his head. "Of course not. So what's that mayor's story?"

"The Davis family is one of the most prominent in Coral Cove. Tyler's grandfather bought up a lot of property, so Tyler has money and thinks he has influence with his little mayor's job. He's all about tourism and money for the town."

"We went to school with him?"

"Oh, yeah. He was class president there, too." She parked the car and sighed. "Okay, happy, smiley faces for Michael."

"I think I can manage that."

When they entered Michael's room, he looked up from his coloring, the tip of his pink tongue lodged in the corner of his mouth. His dark eyes widened for a second, and then he smiled.

The smile made Devon's nose tingle with tears, even if this smile seemed to be directed over her shoulder at Kieran hovering behind her. On some level did Michael sense his father had just walked into the room?

A matching smile curved her lips and she skipped to his bed. "How are you feeling? I missed you."

"Fine. I got to watch TV this morning."

"That's always a big plus when you stay in the hospital. No more coughing?"

"Nope."

"Ready to go home?" Kieran folded down the metal railing and perched on the edge of the bed.

Michael peered at him through lowered lashes and nodded.

With a pounding heart, Devon took a deep breath. "Michael, you like Kieran, don't you?"

Kieran shot her a quick look and then dipped his chin—not that she needed his approval. She'd made a decision and just maybe the news would shake Michael out of his funk. Of course, if the announcement caused him further turmoil, she'd never forgive herself.

"Yeah." Michael's small frame jerked to attention.

"Good…because Kieran is your father."

Chapter Nine

Kieran held his breath. If Michael went ballistic or shut down even further, it would stretch Kieran's nonexistent parenting skills to the snapping point. Had Devon chosen this moment, hoping the news would launch Michael back into the world of the living?

Or had she done it to launch *him* back into the world of the living?

Michael's small hand clutched his red crayon, and then he glanced up quickly. "I know."

Kieran almost slid off the bed as relief poured through his body. Devon had made the right move. If she hadn't told him, Michael would be wondering why they were keeping it a secret.

Devon blew out a noisy breath—must've been holding hers, too—and plopped down next to Kieran on the hospital bed. Her hands trembled as she pleated Michael's covers with agitated fingers.

"Is that okay with you, buddy?" Kieran chucked Michael under the chin with his knuckle, wondering if *buddy* was an okay term. Too corny? Too 1950s? Hell, what did he know?

Michael smiled and nodded. Seemed an understated response to potentially life-changing news, but then the kid, his son, had pretty much been acting like a robot since the moment Kieran had met him. But he'd take the smile.

Devon smoothed a lock of dark hair from Michael's brow, her fingers still shaky. "Okay, then. Let's get you all checked out and you and your father can get to know each other better."

The doctor chose that moment to come in for one last check of Michael's vitals. Raising his brows, his gaze bounced among the three of them. "Everything okay?"

Kieran tweaked Michael's nose to break the tension, and Michael rewarded him with another smile. "Everything's great, Doc. Do your thing so we can get this young man out of here."

As the doctor whipped out his little flashlight and tongue depressor, Kieran pulled Devon into the corridor. "Your instincts were right on with that one. He probably would've been even more confused had we continued to keep it a secret."

"I agree. I'm glad he didn't freak out and withdraw even further into his shell, but I went with my instincts on that one."

"How'd you know he wouldn't?"

She shrugged. "He smiled at you when we came

into the room—at you, not me. His smiles are few and far between these days."

"I'm glad you trusted your parental instincts. I'm going to have to work on those."

"It comes…with time. I'm just sorry that everything's so messed up right now. The way Michael has been questioning me lately about his father, I expected more of a reaction. I'm sorry. It's not the homecoming I had dreamed about."

"At least you'd dreamed about one."

They collected Michael and secured him in his car seat. Kieran had to start somewhere, so he insisted on fiddling with the car seat's straps and buckles himself. Michael helped him by handing him one of the latches.

"You're pretty handy, huh? That's why you're going to go to the hardware store with me." He turned to Devon. "Driver?"

"Luckily there's an outdoor shopping center with a hardware store and a few places for me because I'm going to leave that nuts-and-bolts shopping to you guys." Her gaze wandered to the rearview mirror. "Is that okay with you, Michael?"

Kieran didn't dare turn around. He didn't want to put any pressure on his son, but apparently the idea met with his approval because Devon nodded as she started the car.

As she swung into the large parking lot of the

shopping center, Kieran leaned over and said in a low voice, "Does he sit in the basket?"

"Ask him. Sometimes he likes to for fun and sometimes he'd rather walk."

Kieran plumbed the depths of his addled mind for other scenarios he could encounter on this shopping trip. He didn't trust his judgment to make the right choice when the time came.

He swiped at a trickle of sweat along his hairline. Being a father contained more landmines than an enemy outpost.

Devon nabbed a parking space somewhere between the giant hardware store at the far end of the lot and an equally giant linens store. "Okay, you guys are on your own."

Her simple words sent more fear to his belly than he'd ever encountered as a soldier. But in Michael's state, he proved to be a docile companion, preferring to walk, although he clung to the basket, and agreeing with every one of Kieran's suggestions.

In a short time, Kieran had cruised through the store and picked up the items he'd need to outfit Mrs. Reese's home with enough sensor lighting to pick up a stray beetle. It had better be enough to scare off a killer.

Devon texted him while he was waiting in the check-out line to meet her at the coffee place at the northwest corner of the parking lot. Kieran paid for the purchases and handed Michael two bags to carry. At least Michael seemed physically strong and fit. The mind? They could work on that. They could both work on that.

As he and Michael sauntered to Devon's table, she wore a worried look and had a cell phone pressed to her ear. Kieran's pace quickened along with his pulse.

When Devon noticed their approach, she put up her index finger.

"It sure looks that way, Detective Marquette."

Kieran yanked out a chair for Michael and another for himself. It was the SFPD homicide detective.

Devon shook her head. "I doubt it. Too coincidental, don't you think?"

She paused and rolled her eyes at Kieran. He wished she'd put that thing on speaker, but she probably didn't want to scare Michael.

Devon slammed her frothy coffee drink on the table and gripped the phone with two hands. "Things? What things?"

She then rattled off the address of her mother's house and ended the call. "That was Detective Marquette." She toyed with the straw on her frozen coffee drink, and then dug into her purse. She opened her palm to reveal several coins. "Michael, do you want to toss some coins into the fountain and make a wish? We'll be right here."

He held out his hand and she dumped the change into it.

Kieran watched Michael walk to the fountain, and then turned to Devon. "Everything okay?"

"Detective Marquette is already on his way down."

"That's a good thing."

"Yeah." She drew her bottom lip between her teeth and studied Michael perched on the edge of the fountain chucking coins into the water. "He said he had some things to discuss with me about Mrs. Del Vecchio."

"That's the purpose of the visit, right? That and connecting some dots with these attacks on you."

She shoved the drink away from her. "It's the way he said it. *Things*. Like Mrs. Del Vecchio had something in her past."

"She might. Maybe that's why the killer targeted her." He spread his hands. "So what's the problem?"

"The problem is that I allowed Michael unsupervised visits with her without knowing her past. I could've put him in danger."

Kieran wiped the back of his hand across his mouth. Guess the insecurities about parenthood never ended. If Devon still questioned herself, what chance did he have at getting this right? "She was an old woman. Why would you think there was a problem?"

She flattened her hands on the wrought-iron table and curled her fingers into the gaps. "I don't know—that instinct thing. I should've noticed something. Mrs. Del Vecchio was a little odd, but colorful and harmless...or so I thought."

He covered one of her hands with his. "You don't even know what Marquette is going to say. Stop beating yourself up."

She parted her lips, and he could almost taste the coffee and sweet cream on her mouth. "Kieran..."

The words were lost as Michael approached the table with his hands shoved into his pockets.

"So, did you make some good wishes?"

Michael kicked the toe of his sneaker against the leg of his chair and nodded.

"I hope they all come true." She pointed to the bulging bag that Michael had lugged from the hardware store. "Looks like you're ready for a top secret operation."

"Top secret." Michael climbed into a chair and licked his lips while staring at the see-through plastic cup.

Devon popped the lid off her coffee drink and shoved it over to Michael. "You can have the whipped cream but no coffee."

Michael started poking at the mound of cream with the straw and Devon folded her hands around her cell phone and raised her eyes to Kieran's face.

"So, do you think this top secret operation is going to be successful?"

"I guess we'll find out." Kieran smacked the table. "What do you say, Michael? Are you ready to get operation safe house up and running?"

Two hours later, Kieran stepped back from the house, hands on his hips, and surveyed his handiwork. Who knew putting up lights to catch a killer would bring him one step closer to his son? If Michael was afraid for his mother, afraid for himself, this activity had given him back a little control.

Kieran knew all about feeling helpless and what that could do to your insides.

Devon joined him on the porch. "All done?"

"Yep. I don't think so much as a blade of grass will sway out here without setting off those lights."

"Great. Mom's neighbors are going to love me." She jumped off the bottom step and crouched next to Michael, who was busy studying a line of ants trundling up the driveway. "It's after two o'clock. You must be hungry. I made some sandwiches."

Michael abandoned the ants and scurried into the house, holding up his hand for a quick high five from Kieran on the way inside.

Kieran stared after him. "Seems to be getting his appetite back."

"Seems to be getting a lot back since we told him about you." She put her hand on his arm to stop him from following Michael. "While you guys were working out here, I got a call from Detective Marquette. He's stopping by Coral Cove P.D. first and will be here around four o'clock."

"That's good. Don't worry about it."

"I'm worried about Michael. Seeing Detective Marquette will remind him about Granny Del's death. He'll associate him with that time."

"He still takes naps, right?"

She nodded. "Most of the time."

"After all the excitement of the past few days, he should be ready to crash after he eats. Maybe he'll sleep through the detective's visit."

"The car puts him to sleep. Maybe we can go for a quick drive before Detective Marquette gets here."

He held open the screen door for her. "Let's eat first. I'm starving."

She patted his stomach. "You seem to be getting your appetite back, too."

Her fingers skimmed the waistband of his shorts, and he bit the inside of his cheek. He had appetites, all right, and they included more than a sandwich and an apple.

Devon poured Michael a glass of milk and then stood with the refrigerator door open. "Kieran, would you like lemonade? Iced tea?"

"Water." He pushed back from the table. "I'll get it. Sit down and eat."

While they were eating, Devon dropped the

crust of her sandwich and brushed her fingers together. "I forgot to ask you about the diary. Did you drop it at the house when...when we were there?"

"I must have. I probably dropped it in the library. And I forgot to tell you in all the—" he shot a quick glance at Michael busily dunking cookies in his milk "—excitement that I made out a name on the back cover just before all the...excitement."

"Really?" Devon planted her elbows on the table and sunk her chin in her hands, her eyes shining with anticipation.

"I hate to burst your bubble, but the diary wasn't some old heirloom. The name I saw on the back cover was Marissa St. Regis and a date."

"Oh, not very interesting." She plucked a paper napkin out of the holder on the table and tossed it to Michael. "Wipe your fingers."

"And the date was recent, maybe ten years ago."

"Ten years ago? That's about the time she ran off with Mia's boyfriend. That could be some fascinating reading." She tilted her head toward Michael. "Maybe we should take a drive over there and get it."

Kieran clenched his teeth. He didn't want Devon anywhere near the scene of the shooting. "We'll drive over there, but you stay in the car with Michael and I'll run in and get it."

"Sounds like a plan. We're going to take a drive

to Columbella House, Michael. Do you want to see the house again?"

"Haunted house." Michael covered the lower half of his face with the napkin and peered over the top.

"It's not haunted. Besides, we're not going inside."

Kieran winked at Michael to give a reassurance he didn't feel. *Yeah, ghosts aren't haunting that house, but real, live killers are.*

As Devon drove down Coral Cove Drive, Kieran eased out a breath and rolled his shoulders when he saw a couple gardening outside a house down the street from Columbella. They looked up from their shears and waved.

Devon waved back. "Those are the Vincents. They're friends of your parents."

On the ride over, Michael had drifted off and now his head was tilted and resting against his car seat.

"I guess it worked." Kieran jerked his thumb toward the backseat. "I'll run inside and try to find the diary."

"Okay, hurry. I don't want to get stuck in a long conversation with the Vincents. We need to get back for Detective Marquette."

Kieran slipped out of the car, careful not to slam the door and wake Michael. He crept up the side of the house, lifted the plywood and gained access to the kitchen. Daylight played through the windows, showing him the way with a crisscross pattern of sunlight on the floor.

He edged into the library, darker now with one more plywood window where the bullet had shattered the glass. He knelt on the floor by the desk where he had pulled Devon to safety.

Squinting at the scene with his good eye, his breath hitched. Someone had been here. The sheet over the desk drooped to the floor at an angle. Someone had tucked the leather chair beneath the desk.

Had the cops been back? They'd sent someone to board up the window. Maybe the person who had done that job stepped into the library for some reason.

Crouching forward, he swept his hands across the dusty wood floor, swirls of sunbeams dancing in the shaft of light from the window. Where had he dropped the diary?

He sat back on his heels and surveyed the area. He'd lunged at Devon when he saw the movement at the window. Maybe the book flew out of his hand.

Judging the trajectory, he checked a wider range of the floor, lifting dust covers from the furniture and crawling under tables. Nothing. No red diary.

He rose to his feet, brushed his hands together

and sneezed. It had been a whim anyway, but why would someone take a diary?

He exited the house the same way he had entered and jogged back to the car. His heart stuttered when he saw a man leaning toward the driver's side window. He felt for his weapon until the man stepped back and Kieran recognized him as the gardening neighbor—Mr. Vincent. He was supposed to know him.

He inhaled a lungful of salty sea air and slowed his steps to the car.

"Hey, Kieran. It's great to have you home. Your parents must be ecstatic."

They will be...as soon as I tell them.

Kieran extended his hand. "Mr. Vincent. Good to see you again."

Vincent smacked the roof of the car. "I'll let you folks get going, and I'm RSVPing for the welcome home party right now."

Wouldn't be much of a party without the honoree.

"We'll keep you posted." Kieran dropped onto the passenger seat and exhaled. "I wish I could remember all of these people at first look."

"You'll get there." Devon glanced at his empty hands. "Where's the diary?"

"Gone."

"You can't find it?"

"I mean it's gone. I looked. It's not there."

Devon tilted her head and the sun glimmered along strands of her golden hair. "That's weird. It must've slipped behind something, or maybe one of the cops took it."

"I searched the library thoroughly, and why would one of the cops take it?"

"I don't know." She shifted into Drive and made a U-turn on the street. "The same reason we wanted to have a look."

"He'll probably be as disappointed as you to find out it's from ten years ago instead of a hundred." Kieran buzzed down the window and gulped in the air, trying to clear the dust and the residue of the old house from his lungs.

"Well, it doesn't belong to any of us, but I wonder if Mia would be interested. Ten years ago was about the time her sister disappeared. She might want to be privy to her twin's thought processes at the time."

"Disappeared? I thought you said she ran off with Mia's boyfriend?"

"She did, and they disappeared together. Marissa St. Regis hasn't been back since."

"I gather Mia St. Regis hasn't been back, either."

"No, but she might want to know about the diary. I still have her email address from a few get-togethers the locals arranged. I'll send her a message."

"But we don't have the diary."

"Mia might be able to find it if she ever goes through the house."

He cocked an eyebrow at her. "Are you saying I did a lousy job of searching? I know my vision isn't the best...."

She slugged his arm at the first joke he'd ever made about his eye. "That's not what I meant. Besides, it doesn't much matter now. Michael is sound asleep and he'll sleep through Detective Marquette's visit."

After Kieran had carried Michael to his bed, they didn't have to wait too long for that visit.

Devon invited the detective into the house and introduced him to Kieran.

After shaking his hand with a strong, sure grip, Detective Marquette shrugged out of his suit jacket. "Hope you don't mind, Ms. Reese. It's a lot warmer down here than in the city."

"No surprise there. I'll hang it up for you."

Noting the man's erect posture and crisp movements, Kieran asked, "What branch of the military?"

Marquette's brown face split into a smile. "Marines."

"Green Berets."

"I know. I heard about you, Roarke. Heard about your mission."

"Helluva long mission."

Devon returned to the room, bearing a tray of glasses filled with iced tea. The ice tinkled as she set the tray on the coffee table. Had she just interrupted something between Kieran and Marquette? "Iced tea, Detective?"

"Thanks, I can use it. The local chief is not very hospitable."

Devon grabbed a glass and settled into an armchair, curling her legs beneath her. "Chief Evans is leaving for another department and not too thrilled that I've apparently brought a killer to Coral Cove with me."

Marquette took a sip from his glass and pulled out a well-worn notepad. "Let's talk about that. Someone broke into your car, stole your purse, slashed your tires, threw a Molotov cocktail into a bathroom and then took a couple of potshots at you? Did I miss anything?"

"That about sums it up. I'm a nurse, not an international spy. The only thing out of the ordinary in my life recently has been discovering Mrs. Del Vecchio's body."

That and my dead fiancé showing up on the beach.

Detective Marquette tapped his notepad with a stubby pencil. "What about your brother, Dylan?"

Kieran hunched forward, elbows on his knees. "What about him?"

Devon narrowed her eyes. "He fell off the face

of the earth and then resurfaced recently to tell me he's resigning from the San Jose P.D. and going for the top job here."

"You don't know why he fell off the face of the earth?"

"No, but apparently you do. Spill it."

Marquette lifted an end-tackle-sized shoulder. "Your brother, Ms. Reese, had been working undercover in the gang unit. He almost single-handedly brought down the Fifteenth Street Lords, and then they retaliated by killing a journalist your brother had been working with."

Devon covered her mouth with both hands. Guilt galloped up one side of her body and down the other. She should've known Dylan would have never abandoned her and Michael. "I had no idea."

"I'm sure he didn't want you to know, but it's something to think about. Maybe a few of those gangbangers are looking for another way to strike back at him."

She picked up her sweating glass with a shaky hand and took a gulp. "Who knew my life was so complicated? Do you really think someone could be after me because of Dylan's work?"

"I'm just throwing it out there. Things aren't always as straightforward as they might seem, which brings us back to Mrs. Del Vecchio."

"I didn't see anything that day, Detective Marquette. You guys didn't put out the word that you had a witness or anything, did you?"

"We wouldn't do that, Ms. Reese. One news story specifically stated that we had no witnesses. If Mrs. Del Vecchio's killer is after you, he believes for some reason he has something to fear from you."

She snorted. "That's a good one. He's the one with the Molotov cocktails and guns."

She flicked a gaze toward Kieran. *And I'm the one with the badass pirate keeping watch.*

"You mentioned something about Mrs. Del Vecchio on the phone. Is that what you meant by things not being as simple as they appeared?"

"Yeah, are you ready for this?"

Devon swung her legs out from under her and planted her feet on the floor. "Yep."

"Mrs. Del Vecchio's husband, Johnny, was a criminal and a bank robber. They called him Johnny Del. He died in prison and rumor has it he left a bundle of cash in hiding with his widow."

Chapter Ten

Devon curled her bare toes against the Persian throw rug on the floor and dug her fingernails into the arms of the chair. Was this some kind of sick joke?

"A-are you kidding me?"

Detective Marquette held up his spatulate hands. "No lie."

Kieran swore. "Is that why she was murdered?"

"We think so. Before the autopsy results came back, we wondered at the cause of death. At first we thought she'd been strangled because of the marks on her neck, but she actually drowned. And we think it was accidental."

"You think her murder was accidental?" Devon rubbed her arms, trying to erase the goose bumps.

"It looks that way. Why drown her when you already have your hands wrapped around her throat? We think the dunking in the sink full of water was a means for extracting information."

Devon clasped her hands at her own throat.

"They were asking her questions and then dunking her head in the water when she wouldn't answer?"

"We think so."

"How awful. And the questions?"

"They probably wanted to know what Johnny Del did with the money from the last bank heist."

"'They'? Do you think more than one person killed her?" Kieran shoved forward to perch on the edge of the chair, his knees meeting Devon's.

"We don't know. It doesn't seem likely since you heard just one person that day, Ms. Reese."

She pressed her bouncing knees against Kieran's steady leg. "I didn't hear anyone, just a door slam."

Detective Marquette wrapped his hands around his glass and downed the rest of his drink. "How's that little boy of yours?"

"He's still shaken up, but—" she shot a glance at Kieran "—he's getting better every day."

"That's good to hear. He must've been close to Mrs. Del Vecchio for her death to affect him like that."

"Yeah, he called her..." Devon smacked her hand on the coffee table "...Johnny Del."

The detective's brows shot up. "He called the old lady 'Johnny Del'?"

"No, but she had him call her Granny Del. Close enough, isn't it?" She dragged her hands through her hair and tugged at the roots. "How could I have allowed that friendship?"

Kieran reached over and squeezed her knee. "How were you supposed to know that sweet, little Granny Del was some bank robber's moll?"

"That's just it, Kieran. Granny Del was a bit unusual. She encouraged him to sneak down to see her. She'd tell Michael cops and robbers stories and pirate stories, and somehow the robbers and pirates always turned out to be the good guys."

Detective Marquette barked out a laugh, and then held up his hands. "I'm sorry. It's just funny to think that the old gal never changed her spots. From what I read about her, she never once ratted out Johnny Del."

"Apparently, she stayed true to him until the end, dying rather than giving up his secret stash… or her secret stash."

The detective rose and stretched his big frame. "I'm going to hit the road. I plan to stay in touch with the CCPD about your situation out here, and I'm going to put together a six-pack of Johnny Del's old partners."

"Looking at a six-pack of mug shots of Johnny Del's old cronies isn't going to help, Detective. I didn't see anyone from the laundry room that day." She made a crisscross over her heart. "I promise."

"I know that. I'm hoping you can make a connection between the pictures and someone lurking around Coral Cove."

"And my brother? Are you going to check that out, too?" She slipped Detective Marquette's jacket off the hanger in the closet and handed it to him.

"I will, although I don't think he's going to be too happy I let you in on his secret." He draped the jacket over his arm. "I figure I'm leaving you in good hands."

"Ha! Chief Evans?"

He leveled a finger at Kieran. "No. That fully capable Green Beret."

Devon sent Detective Marquette on his way with a can of cold soda for his three-hour drive back to the city.

Crossing her arms, she leaned against the porch post, watching his taillights disappear around the corner. She blinked her eyes. "I can't believe Dylan didn't tell me about his operation."

Kieran's hand brushed up her back and settled on her neck. "As a cop's daughter, you know it would've been impossible for him to tell you."

She shivered and the sun hadn't even dipped into the ocean yet. "His distance over the past few years hurt me…and Michael. When Michael was a toddler, Dylan was the closest thing he had to a father."

"But he wasn't a father. That's my job now."

"I know you're trying hard, and I appreciate it."

"Too hard?"

She gazed into Kieran's single dark eye edged with uncertainty. She'd never seen this man anything but confident—on the football field, in the classroom, in the bedroom. Even returning home with a damaged eye and an even more damaged memory, he'd seemed in control. One little four-year-old boy had sapped that assurance.

"You could never try too hard with Michael. Just continue doing what you're doing—include him, talk to him, share with him, but…"

"But what?" The light pressure on her neck turned to a caress.

She clenched her muscles, her body stiffening. She didn't want to put Kieran on the spot, but he asked and she owed him the truth. She gathered a deep breath in her lungs. "I don't want Michael to be disappointed. If he finds a father only to lose him…"

With slight pressure on her shoulders, he turned her to face him. "I'm not going to abandon Michael."

What about me? The question hovered on her lips, but she was afraid to hear the answer. Right now, his promise to Michael had to be enough.

Her cell phone buzzed and she checked the display, grateful for the distraction. "It's Elena."

She hit the speaker button and answered. "Hi,

Elena. Kieran's here and Michael isn't. You're on speaker."

"Hello, Devon, Kieran. Michael wasn't with you during the shooting incident, was he?"

"Thank God, no. We had to bring him to the hospital last night for a cough he developed. We dropped by Kieran's parents' place and saw lights at Columbella, and that's when the shooting ensued."

"That poor boy. Is he okay now?"

"He's fine." Devon wrapped an arm around the wooden post of the porch, even though she would've preferred holding on to Kieran. "Elena, we told him. Kieran and I told Michael that Kieran is his father."

Elena paused. "How did he take it?"

"He said he already knew."

Elena laughed. "The wisdom of children."

"Did he say anything in the session about Kieran?"

"He just nodded when I asked if he liked him." Elena cleared her throat. "He probably got enough signals from you that Kieran was a special man."

Devon's cheeks heated and she dipped her head to hide them from Kieran's intent gaze. "I suppose so. Is there anything we need to know about the session? Anything you can tell us?"

"Not at this point. Michael's a disturbed little boy, Devon, but I don't have to tell you that."

Devon sagged against the wooden pillar, and Kieran wrapped an arm around her. The heavy drape of his forearm caused her to straighten her shoulders. She had to be strong for Michael.

Kieran whispered in her ear. "Tell her about Granny Del."

"There's something else you should know before your next session with Michael. The SFPD detective working the case came down this afternoon with some interesting information about Mrs. Del Vecchio."

She told Elena about Johnny Del and the missing money.

"Wow, what a colorful past. You don't know what kinds of things she was telling Michael.… And no, none of it is your fault. That's an interesting twist, and I'll see if I can get Michael to open up about some of the things he talked about with Granny Del."

"Okay, so ten o'clock tomorrow morning?"

"Yes, and Kieran?"

"Yeah?" Devon could almost feel Kieran's hard muscles coil and prepare for battle.

"I've reserved the time immediately following Michael's appointment for you. Interested?"

"Sure."

"Good. You two have a safe evening. I actually have a date tonight."

"Have a good time, and thanks, Elena." Devon

ended the call and slid the phone into the front pocket of her shorts.

Kieran took one step down and crossed his arms. "Why did I think Dr. Estrada was married, or is the date with her husband?"

"Elena's husband passed away three years ago—heart attack out of the blue."

"A lot of stuff can happen—out of the blue."

The screen door banged behind them and Devon jumped.

"Mommy?"

Michael stood on the porch rubbing his eyes.

She tousled his hair. "Did you have a good nap?"

"Uh-huh."

At least no nightmares had interrupted his sleep. "How about a bath and then some dinner?"

Michael gazed up at the eaves, his eyes wide, and Devon's heart rate accelerated. Was there something up there that scared him? Would danger continue to lurk in every nook and cranny of Michael's existence?

Kieran crouched beside Michael. "It's too light right now. The sensor lights will start working when it's dark."

Michael grinned and Devon's pounding heart did a double backflip. Lord, had she ever missed that grin. Truth was she loved it because it was a carbon copy of Kieran's. Maybe she'd get a double reward and see the grin echoed on Kieran's face.

Nope—just that little twist of the lips. Maybe his son could teach Kieran how to smile again.

"Has Michael ever been to Neptune's Catch?"

"You remember that restaurant?"

Kieran shrugged. "Of course I do. Friends of the family own that place, and they have the best calamari around."

"Camilari?"

"Exactly." Kieran poked Michael in the back. "Little deep-fried squid. Have you ever eaten a squid before, Michael?"

His dark eyes took up half his face as he shook his head.

Kieran tsked and shook a finger at Devon. "You haven't taken Michael to Fisherman's Wharf to eat squid?"

"I'm not a complete failure. He's had crab and clam chowder in a bread bowl."

Michael's gaze darted between her and Kieran, a half smile on his face, not sure whether to be anxious about their bantering or happy.

Devon tugged on his ear. "Kieran and I are just joking around. Do you want to try some cala- mari?"

"Yeah, camilari."

"You got it. Camilari all around."

It was almost seven o'clock before they left the

Roarkes' house and hit the coast highway. Having a 24-7 bodyguard and a single car slowed down daily operations. Bath and shower at her place, followed by shower at his place.

But she wasn't complaining, even though they could save time and water by showering together.

As she drove toward the more touristy area of Coral Cove, the lights on the shore, dotted with restaurants and bed and breakfasts, twinkled. They'd missed the sunset, so maybe they'd be able to nab a window seat if the crowds had dispersed after the sun went down.

She didn't have to worry. The owners of the restaurant treated Kieran like a conquering hero, and placed them at the best window seat with an unobstructed view of the Pacific.

When the calamari arrived, Michael poked at it suspiciously, especially the ones with the little tentacles. But when Kieran dipped one of the critters into a spicy, red sauce and popped it into his mouth, Michael followed suit.

"Do you like it?" Kieran's hand hovered over the plate, ready to nab another one.

With his mouth full, Michael nodded his head.

Devon sighed as she sipped her one and only glass of wine for the evening. This felt right. Then she gulped some ice water. *Better not get used to it.*

Kieran had promised to be a part of Michael's

life and she believed him, but he hadn't included her in his little vision of the future...yet. Could she change his mind? Seduce him?

She'd never use Michael to hook him, but she wasn't above employing a little va-va-voom. Did she even have any of that left? Guess she'd better find out. With the sensor lights manning the exterior of the house, Kieran would be free to man the interior.

And then she'd be free to man him.

Kieran tapped her wine glass. "Slow down. You're driving."

"Huh?" She blinked her eyes. "I do not get tipsy on one glass of wine, especially after eating a boatload of calamari and a bowl of cioppino."

His eye narrowed. "You had a silly grin on your face."

"Did I?" She kicked off her sandal and wiggled her toes against his ankle. "Just happy to be here."

He'd just taken a sip of water and now he was choking and spewing it into his napkin.

She chewed her bottom lip. Maybe she had the va-va but was missing the voom.

"Devon, Kieran. What a surprise to see you here."

Devon jerked her head to the side and met Elena's shining, dark eyes. "Oh, h-hello."

She stammered to a stop, not sure of the protocol. Elena was her friend, but she was also

Michael's therapist and typically Elena didn't socialize with her clients or at least she didn't acknowledge them in public.

A man about Elena's age had her hand tucked into the crook of his arm.

Elena smiled. "Sam, this is Devon and Kieran, and their son, Michael. This is Sam."

They shook hands, and Michael slouched in his chair. Elena tapped his shoulder. "Hello, Michael."

"Hi."

Elena beamed at him as if he'd just recited the Gettysburg Address, but a verbal greeting was better than his customary nods. Had to celebrate every little bit of progress.

They chatted about the food and the view before Elena and her date moved on to their table.

"So that's Dr. Estrada's date." Kieran dumped the rest of his beer from the bottle into his glass.

"Seems like a nice enough guy."

"Must be hard to move on after losing a spouse."

"Or a fiancé."

His gaze sharpened on her face, but he chose to ignore the comment. Instead, he asked Michael if he wanted dessert.

They all shared a hot fudge brownie sundae, with Michael doing most of the damage, and then headed for home…for Devon's mother's house just to make things more complicated.

When they got out of the car, Michael insisted

on checking out all the sensor lights. He ran across the front yard, crept around the side of the house and even slipped through the side gate to the back-yard. Everywhere he ran, bright lights followed him.

"Okay, Michael, I think they all work."

He scampered inside the house, and Devon got him ready for bed. When he was all tucked in, she leaned over and whispered in his ear. "Do you want Kieran to come and say good-night?"

Michael's dark eyes lit up, and Devon poked her head out of his room. "Kieran, would you like to say good-night to Michael?"

He appeared in the hallway as if he'd been wait-ing. "Yeah, I'd like that."

Devon scooted over to make room for Kieran on Michael's bed and swallowed hard. She'd never had to make room for anyone in Michael's life before.

Kieran held up his fist for a bump and Michael touched his knuckles. "Good night, Michael. Thanks for helping me with the lights."

Michael snuggled into his bed and turned his face to his pillow. In a muffled voice, he said, "I like camilari."

"Yeah, me, too."

Devon dimmed Michael's light to a low glow and left his door ajar. That was the easy part. Now who was going to tuck *her* in?

"Another beer?"

"No, thanks. I don't drink much these days."

"I'm glad you're going to keep the appointment with Elena tomorrow. I think she can help you remember even more."

Kieran stuffed his hands in his pockets. "It's not just the…"

She waited, but his words trailed into nothingness. Everything between them was trailing into nothingness. Except Michael. She had to be grateful for that and put an end to these selfish feelings. Would she rather have a father for Michael or a husband and lover for herself?

The stubborn little voice taking up residence in the back of her brain shouted, *Both. Why can't I have both?*

"Do you want to watch TV?" She gestured toward the dark screen. "Or do you want to turn in? You must be exhausted. I made up the bed in Dylan's old room."

"I'm going to sleep out here."

"On the couch?"

"Yeah."

"I think those floodlights out there are enough to scare off the most determined stalker."

"I'd rather sleep here."

Of course you would, you stubborn man. Why be comfortable? Why relax? Why give into this sexual tension between us?

"Okay. I'll bring you a blanket and pillow. I'm going to read for a while." She pulled the blanket from Dylan's bed and grabbed the pillow. Grinding her teeth, she folded the blanket on the couch and dropped the pillow on top.

Then she punched the pillow. "Good night. Sweet dreams."

Kieran's brown eye grew even darker, and the lines on the sides of his mouth deepened. "Good night, Devon."

After Devon washed her face and brushed her teeth, she flopped across her bed. What was that last look all about? Had he been angry that she'd shown her frustration?

He'd have to accept the fact that she wasn't some celestial being full of light and forgiveness. That image may have gotten him through his imprisonment, but it had no place in the real world. Not in her world.

The murmur of the TV floated down the hallway as Devon folded open her book. If Kieran were so concerned about watching her back, he'd better not try to go without sleep for a second night in a row. He'd be useless.

Her lids drifted over her eyes as she pictured Kieran standing in her living room, the black patch hiding one window to his soul, every line of his body hard and ready, every line on his face harsh and uncompromising.

Kieran Roarke would never be useless.

She sighed and slouched farther into her bed, training her eyes on the page of the book, shaking off thoughts of the dangerous man with the eye patch camped out on her couch.

She read for another hour, or at least she stared at the same few pages for over an hour as she strained her ears for any little sound from the other room. It wasn't like she expected him to charge into her bedroom demanding his conjugal rights…or whatever rights he had as a former fiancé.

She didn't expect it, but she wanted it.

Sighing again, she flipped the page of her book to show some progress. Her eyelids grew heavy. Her grip on the paperback slackened. Her head tilted toward her shoulder.

Her body jerked. She sat up, and her book tumbled to the floor. Her gaze shifted to the illuminated numbers on her alarm clock. Two o'clock.

She pressed a hand against her chest where her heart was pounding as if she'd just run a marathon. Something had awakened her. Her gaze tracked to the bedroom window, the curtains drawn tightly across a closed and locked window despite the warmth of the day.

Her fingers curled into the covers and she held her breath as if that could sharpen her hearing.

Because that was it. She'd heard a noise that had jolted her out of a restless sleep.

There—a moan. No, a growl. A tortured, feral sound that ripped her heart out of her chest.

Throwing the covers back, she swung her legs out of bed. She blinked, adjusting her eyes to the darkness, and then shuffled across the room to the door.

She cracked it open. A muted, blue light glowed from the living room. Had the noise come from the TV? She pushed open the door and tiptoed down the hallway.

She poked her head around the corner. Kieran, shirtless, boxers hanging low on his hips, raised his head from the hands covering his face, his patchless eye a slit of gleaming light in the darkness of his visage.

Holding out one trembling hand, Devon whispered. "Kieran?"

His body tensed. He took a step forward.

"Kieran, are you okay? I heard some…moaning. Are you in pain?"

Air hissed out between his teeth. His long fingers curled into fists at his sides.

He must be in excruciating pain. "Do you need some ibuprofen? I'm sure I have something stronger."

All at once, Kieran was beside her. His eyes darkened to bits of obsidian—right before he wrapped his hands around her throat.

Chapter Eleven

Fingernails clawed at his wrists. If he squeezed harder, he could vanquish his captor, get away, go home, find his angel.

"Kieran!"

Her voice called out to him. Desperate. Panicked. Choking.

His gaze focused on his prey, the blond hair spilling across his hands. Wide, blue eyes pleading with him. Soft lips formed into an *O*.

Devon. He wrenched the brutal hands from her slender throat. Rage and confusion pounded through his bloodstream. He stumbled back, clenching his fists and wrapping his arms around his body. An anguished cry surged from his belly and he bellowed like a wounded animal.

He continued lurching backward until he pinned himself in the far corner of the room. He stood like an animated statue, his chest heaving, the breath rasping through his lungs, his teeth grinding in rage at the animal he'd become.

Devon, looking more like an angel than ever with the light from the TV illuminating her from behind, extended her arms. Tears sparkled in her eyes and she took a tentative step forward.

"No!" Kieran thrust out his hands, warding her off, willing her to keep a safe distance.

"Kieran."

"Stay away. Don't come near me."

She took another step and the filmy nightgown she wore swayed around her body. "It was a nightmare, Kieran. It's over now. I know you'd never..."

"Hurt you? Kill you?" He forced the words from his dry mouth where they left a bitter taste like bile. "That's exactly what I tried to do."

"You're not dreaming now." She continued her progress toward him, gliding along the floor like a spirit. "I'm not afraid of you."

He laughed and it came out like a snarl. "You should be."

"You're Kieran Roarke. I'm not afraid of Kieran Roarke."

His muscles unclenched. His arms hung at his sides. He slid down the wall until he crouched on the floor, his shoulders slumping forward. "But who's Kieran Roarke?"

A rustle of silk. A whiff of jasmine. And she was on the floor beside him. Her cool, delicate fingers brushed the hair from his eyes. "He's a man of courage and integrity. He's the father of my child."

Anxiety pumped another load of adrenaline into his system, and his head shot up. "Michael. Where's Michael?"

"He's safe in his bed…thanks to you." Her light fingers pressed against his temples. "You saved our lives in that bathroom, and you saved my life at Columbella House. That's the Kieran Roarke I know."

"And the one who just tried to kill you?" He closed his eyes, drawing in a long breath through his flared nostrils.

"That's an aberration. A stumbling block on the way to your full recovery."

"Helluva stumbling block. I'd call that a boulder."

She half-laughed, half-sobbed, and he opened his eyes, his gaze zeroing in on the red marks on her neck. The evidence of his brutality punched him in the gut.

He raised one finger, willing it to hold steady as he traced a pinkish welt on her throat. Her pulse jumped beneath the pad of his finger.

"God, I'm sorry. I'm so sorry."

She pressed her fingers against his lips. "Shh."

He kissed her fingertips and cinched her wrist with two fingers. Then he pressed his lips against the palm of her hand. He stretched out his legs and pulled her into his lap.

She straddled him, the hem of her skimpy nightgown hitching up to her shapely thighs. She wound her arms around his neck, shifting slightly toward him, so close he could see a small pulse beat in her lower lip.

The steady throb hypnotized him, and his own lips tingled with anticipation. He wanted to draw her nearer, thread his hands through her hair and bring her in for a kiss. But his fear of touching her head or the back of her neck paralyzed him.

He shrugged his shoulders off the wall, leaning forward. She got the hint and pulled him toward her. When their lips met, a fire ignited in his body and sizzled along every nerve ending.

She parted her mouth and sighed into his. With his hands still at his sides, he tilted his head, angling to seal his lips across hers. He wouldn't make love to her. He couldn't, even though his lower body raged against the common sense that prevailed in his head.

As he deepened the kiss, a bright light blazed through the window. He blinked.

Devon gasped and slid from his lap. "The sensor lights."

Cursing, he scrambled to his feet and dragged his jeans from the back of the couch. He hopped on one foot and then the other, stuffing his legs into the pants. He reached beneath the couch for the .45 and shivered. Could he be trusted with this weapon in the dead of night when the nightmares took possession of him body and soul?

"Wait here." He crowded Devon away from the front door.

He charged onto the porch, weapon drawn. A skittering noise near the bushes bordering one side of the house drew his attention. He landed on the grass, the damp blades sticking to his bare feet, jabbing between his toes.

Leveling the gun in front of him with two hands, he swung it toward the rattling twigs. Then he took aim at…an opossum.

The rat-like marsupial glared at him, its beady eyes iridescent in the floodlights. Its nose twitched once before it burrowed into the bushes, probably heading for the sand dunes beyond the tract of houses.

"What is it, Kieran?" Devon had thrown on a terry cloth robe, hiding all her silky temptations. She hovered on the porch, legs crossed and one foot on top of the other.

"An opossum."

"Ugh. I hate those things. At least we know the lights work."

A window next door scraped open and a voice yelled into the night. "Turn off those damned lights or I'll call the cops."

Devon giggled, and Kieran ducked back inside the house, pulling her with him.

"The lights work, and your mom has sensitive neighbors. That should be enough to ward off any intruders." He shoved the loaded weapon beneath the couch. "Now get back to bed and try to get some sleep."

Dropping her eyelashes, she tugged at the sash around her waist. "D-do you need company? I know you're not going back to sleep."

"One of us better be wide awake and alert for Michael tomorrow."

"Are you feeling okay, Kieran? Could you use an ibuprofen, aspirin, a drink?"

"I'll settle for an old movie. How about you? Is your neck okay?"

She twisted her head from side to side. "Seems to be in working order."

"Good night, then." He settled on the couch as Devon marched toward the hallway, her gait stiff. He whispered to her ramrod straight back. "I'm sorry…my love."

DEVON STRETCHED AND squinted at the sunshine sneaking through the gap between her bedroom curtains. Once inside, the rays had taken up residence in a thin line that pointed an accusing finger at her bed. Her head lolled to the side, and she swiped at the alarm clock, its numbers facing away from her.

She huffed out a breath and rubbed the sleep from the corners of her eyes. Michael had never allowed her to sleep this late before. He'd come charging into her bedroom, full of some scheme or plan for the day.

Of course, that was before Granny Del's murder. Granny Del, the bank robber's widow. Her pulse picked up to a rapid staccato beat. Even after Mrs. Del Vecchio's murder, Michael never slept this late.

She scrambled out of bed and dragged her ratty robe over her nightgown. While wearing her sexiest nightie, she'd failed miserably at seducing Kieran last night, so she might as well be warm and comfortable.

She twisted the handle of the door, which she'd left ajar last night. Had Kieran shut her door in some misguided attempt to protect her from him? Even when he'd had his hands around her throat, she'd known he could never hurt her.

Pots and pans clanged and wisps of steam carried buttery smells throughout the house. She turned the corner and surveyed the kitchen, the sink piled with dirty dishes, batter dripping a bumpy path down the cabinet door.

Michael, standing on a chair at the counter, turned to wave floury fingers in her direction.

Kieran lifted the lid of the waffle iron and speared a fluffy, golden sphere. He dropped it onto a plate piled with identical mates and gave Michael a high five. "Another perfect waffle."

"I hope your cooking is better than your cleaning." She braced her knuckles on her hips.

"Cleaning?" Kieran waved a hand at the sink. "We're master chefs. We don't worry about cleaning."

"I suppose I can strike a deal with you." She approached Michael and dabbed a smudge of chocolate at the corner of his mouth. "What's on the menu?"

Kieran pointed his fork at the steaming plate. "Waffles—chocolate chip or blueberry."

"Mmm, sounds yummy. I can definitely clean up in exchange for a few waffles." She grabbed some plates from the cupboard, throwing a sidelong glance at Kieran. If he had stayed awake the rest of the night, he didn't look any worse for it. Sure, black stubble dotted his chin and his longish hair stuck out at odd angles, but he'd always looked best as his rugged, natural self. Although he cleaned up pretty nicely, too.

He took the plates from her hands, brushing her fingers with his. "Are you still tired? Thought I'd let you sleep in."

"I appreciate it." She shook her head, dislodging the visions of Kieran from her brain. He didn't want her. He'd made that clear last night…after the kiss. After his terrifying sleepwalking incident.

Did he think he could tell her what to do for her own good? She had her own plans, and they didn't include tiptoeing around the man she loved because of a few bad dreams.

Did she still love him?

She watched him return to Michael. He gave that twisted grin as he scooped his son from the chair and carried him to the table under one arm. Hell yes, she still loved him, and she planned to fight for that love.

Fifteen minutes later, Michael stuffed the last forkful of waffle into his mouth and licked his lips.

Devon pointed to the napkin in his lap, hanging toward the floor. "Use that, and then get dressed and brush your teeth. You're going to visit Dr. Elena today."

She studied her son's face for any anxiety, or any more anxiety than he'd been exhibiting since the murder, but he just dragged the napkin across his mouth and dropped it on his plate before pushing back from the table.

Kieran started running water in the sink for the dishes and squirted a line of yellow liquid into the stream from the faucet. "I need to brush my teeth, too. I'll meet you in the bathroom, Michael."

"Go now." Devon flicked her fingers at him. "I'll take care of the dishes."

As Kieran turned to follow Michael, Devon put a hand on his forearm. "Maybe you should think about keeping some of your stuff here so we don't have to keep running over to your parents' place every morning."

The muscles in his arm tensed, creating rippling cords beneath her fingers. "I'm not sure that's a good idea. Last night…"

"Last night you had a nightmare."

"I almost strangled you. God knows what I would've done to Michael if I'd come upon him in his bed."

She swiped her fingers through the air as if wiping away his words. "I don't believe you'd harm either one of us."

He reached out and the suddenness of the movement caused her to flinch backward. With his eyelid half closed he traced a line on her throat. "But I did harm you."

"You stopped when you woke up. It's not something you would do in a conscious state."

"You don't know that. Hell, I don't know that."

Her pulse pumped beneath the pad of his finger, sending hot-blooded anger coursing through her veins. She shoved her index finger against his solid chest. "I do know that. You may have lost your memory, Kieran, but I still have mine. You wouldn't hurt anyone you lov…cared about. It's not in you."

They stood almost nose to nose, in each other's face. A muscle twitched in his tightened jaw, and Devon could almost hear his teeth grinding.

"You don't know what's in me anymore, Devon. I'm a changed man."

"In your mind." She rapped on her head with her knuckles. "Stop saying it, stop trying to convince yourself. You're the same man. You did what you had to do to survive."

"If you knew…"

A high-pitched scream cut off Kieran's words, and they both jerked their heads around at the same time.

Michael, framed in the kitchen entryway, hands pressed against his ears, screamed again, his mouth a gaping hole in his face.

The sound plunged a dagger in Devon's heart and she spun around and fell to her knees in front of him. She gathered him in her arms. "It's okay, Michael. Everything's okay. Kieran and I were just talking."

"Oh, great." Kieran lunged for the kitchen faucet, almost slipping on the water that had dripped to the floor from the overflowing sink.

Devon left him to clean up that mess while she carried Michael to his bedroom to clean up another kind of mess. How could they be so insensitive to argue in front of him? He'd just discovered his father, and now he had the tension of arguing parents. He didn't need tension right now.

She sat on the edge of his bed and snuggled him into her lap. At least he'd dropped his hands from his ears. "It's okay. Kieran and I were just talking about something important. We're not mad at each other."

"Daddy."

Devon's heart almost stopped beating in her chest. She swallowed a huge lump in her throat. "That's right. Daddy."

"Did I hear my name?"

Kieran stepped into the room, dwarfing the pint-size furniture, a wet dish towel bunched in his hands. "Sorry your mom and I got carried away. Grown-ups do that sometimes. You can talk to Dr. Elena today about how that made you feel."

Michael shook his head from side to side.

Kieran sat next to Devon on the bed, and the mattress dipped, forcing her and Michael to slide toward him.

"You know, you can tell Dr. Elena everything. That's what I'm going to do. I'm going to see her right after you, and I'm going to tell her everything that's bothering me."

"Your eye?" Michael pointed to his own eye.

"Yep. I'm going to tell her about my eye and about all kinds of other things."

Tears pricked behind Devon's lids as she met Kieran's gaze above Michael's head. He was going to try to get his nightmares under control. Maybe Michael had reminded him that he needed to make the effort instead of just accepting that he was some kind of monster.

Kieran sprang off the bed. "We'd better get going if we want to make it to Dr. Elena's office on time."

Devon swung by Kieran's place, and a smile curved her lips when he jogged down the porch steps with a black duffel bag slung over one shoulder.

She popped her trunk from inside the car, and he loaded the bag in the back.

Cruising into downtown, Devon parked the car on the other side of the office buildings, away from the burned-out restrooms. If Michael associated Elena's office with the bombing of the bathroom, he didn't show it.

They climbed up the back stairs and pushed through the office door. Elena waved them in while she continued talking to a man, his shoulder propped up against the inner office door. When he turned, Devon recognized him as Elena's date from last night.

He gave a brief nod and turned back to Elena. "I'll see you later."

He sidled out of the room without acknowledging them further, most likely trying to honor the confidentiality of Elena's doctor-patient relationship. Guess the cat was out of the bag now that at least one of them was Elena's client.

"Nice to see you again, Michael." Elena smiled at Michael and jerked her chin at the closed door. "That was Sam from last night. He moved into the office a few doors down.... Accountant."

"My session with Michael is one hour today, so you can wait in here or take a walk."

Kieran grabbed a magazine from the rack and settled into a chair. "We'll wait in here today."

Devon took a position in the corner of a love seat and said, "We'll be right out here, Michael."

Elena ushered Michael into the office while Devon slid a magazine from the table and flipped through it for several minutes. She glanced up several times, but Kieran seemed intent on his wildlife magazine.

Finally, she tossed the magazine onto the cushion beside her. "So, do you think he's telling her all about his awful parents and how they were arguing this morning?"

Without looking up from his reading material, Kieran said, "I hope so. That's the point, isn't it?"

Devon chewed on her bottom lip. "We weren't even raising our voices, were we? It didn't seem that bad to me."

"For us it was a tense discussion. For Michael—"

he shrugged "—who knows what was going through his head?"

Kieran still had his nose buried in the magazine, so Devon tried reading hers again, her ears tuned to every sound from Elena's inner sanctum. She and Kieran had decided to wait for Michael in the office today, but being right outside that door made her more nervous than being away from the office.

The outer door inched open, and Kieran jerked his magazine down to peer over the top.

With her heart pounding, Devon raised her brows at him, as he patted the inside pocket of his jacket where he'd stowed his weapon. The door slowly eased open. Sam poked his head through the crack and Devon released a pent-up breath.

"I'm sorry. I think I left my card key to the tenant underground parking garage in here."

"Is this it?" Kieran peeled a white, plastic card from the glass-topped table next to him and held it up between two long fingers.

"Thanks." Sam stepped forward and took the card. "I was hoping it was out here. I need to get my car out of the garage, but of course I wouldn't have disturbed Dr. Estrada while she was with a client."

After he snapped the door behind him, Devon shrugged. "Well, I guess he knows which one of us is Elena's patient now."

"Do you care?"

"Not really. I think it's a lot harder for therapists in small towns to keep that confidentiality thing going."

He folded back his magazine. "She's dating the guy. Don't you think she's going to tell him everything anyway?"

"Elena's ethical. I don't think so." She wedged her feet on the table in front of her. "Are you concerned about that?"

"I figure everyone in town has gotta know I have issues after being imprisoned for that long." He pointed to the magazine. "I want to finish this article before Michael comes out."

Devon jumped up and paced the small outer office. Several minutes and three turns around the carpet later, the door swung open and a smiling Michael, clutching a lollipop, exited with Elena close on his heels.

"Until next time, Michael."

He galloped toward Devon and held up his candy. The galloping was more in line with Michael's typical mode of movement than the floating he'd been doing lately. Galloping was a good sign.

Kieran stood up and stretched. "My turn now."

Michael walked to Kieran and tugged on his pocket. When Kieran looked down, Michael held up his lollipop still in its wrapper.

"That's okay, Michael. You keep that one for yourself and I'll get my own from Dr. Elena."

Kieran turned at the door. "You're going to wait here, right?"

"We'll be here." Devon patted the side of her large bag. "I brought a few things to occupy Michael while we wait, and Elena has a toy chest in the closet."

Kieran and Elena disappeared into her office, and Devon sighed and slumped in one of the chairs. Elena had to help Kieran overcome these nightmares or he'd never trust himself at night alone with her and Michael.

She unzipped her bag and pulled out a puzzle and an easy reader. Michael had been working on sounding out letters before the murder. She held up both. "Which one?"

He pointed to the puzzle and she opened the box and dumped the chunky pieces out on the table for him. He sat cross-legged in front of the table and lined up the pieces in order according to color.

Devon grabbed the celebrity gossip magazine again since that's about all her mind could handle right now. She didn't hear any agonizing screams from the office, so maybe Elena hadn't put Kieran under today.

A half an hour into the session, Devon's cell phone chirped once. She slipped it out of her pocket and checked the display—a text message from Detective Marquette. Her breath quickened as she punched a button to read the entire message.

Can't talk in a mtg with cops. Meet me in 15 min in alley behind pizza place under blue awning.

What was Detective Marquette still doing in town? Devon checked the time on her phone and glanced at the closed door. There was only one pizza place in Coral Cove, Vinnie's Pizza, near the police station.

Kieran didn't want her out and about on her own, but she had her pepper spray and she *was* meeting a detective. He must have something new to tell her about Mrs. Del Vecchio's murder, or maybe Chief Evans had divulged something to Detective Marquette about the threats against her.

She scrambled through her purse for a pen and a piece of paper. She found the receipt for her tires and scribbled a note on the back, giving Kieran her location for the meeting with Detective Marquette.

She slid the note between the door and the doorjamb, propping it against the door handle, and then leaned over the table where Michael was playing. "We're going to meet a friend by the pizza place and then maybe Kier…Daddy can meet us there for lunch when he's done."

Michael helped her sweep the puzzle pieces into the box, and they left the office. The pizza place was close enough to walk there in ten minutes, so Devon grabbed Michael's hand and joined the tourists milling along Coral Cove's main drag. Safety in numbers.

She spotted the red-and-white-striped awning of Vinnie's up ahead and knew they had an identical awning in the back on the alley it shared with the police station and a few other Main Street shops.

Marquette had probably parked in the back and wanted to meet with her before he drove back to the city. Must be something he didn't want the Coral Cove P.D. to hear.

She turned the corner of the street before Vinnie's and headed into the alley where a breeze ruffled the ends of her hair. The buildings on the east side blocked the sun, creating a cool, shaded refuge from the heat.

A car crawled toward her, and she swept Michael up in her arms and sidled along the brick facade of the buildings. The blue minivan cruised past and turned onto Main Street.

Scaffolding blocked Devon's way, so she stepped back into the middle of the alley again. Workers had been replacing the bricks along the tops of the buildings in this row and the red slate tile roofs.

She strode toward Vinnie's red awning and glanced both ways as she parked herself and Michael under the flapping canvas. She must've beat Detective Marquette out of his meeting. She zeroed in on the beige door, which led into the back of the police station farther down the alley.

Another couple of pedestrians passed, using the alley to head into the back door of another business. At least Detective Marquette had picked a fairly populated place for their meeting, or maybe he thought Kieran would be with them.

Would the detective have called her out for a meeting if he had known she'd be solo? She rolled her shoulders back a few times, and smiled at a woman pushing a stroller through the alley toward the park on the other end. It wasn't as if this was some deserted spot in the dead of night.

As the woman and the stroller turned out of the alley, Devon licked her lips, her gaze darting back and forth. Maybe it wasn't a deserted spot in the dead of night, but she wished Marquette would hurry up or she'd go into the police station to get him…whether he wanted this meeting hush-hush or not.

KIERAN FELT BETTER already, and he hadn't even undergone hypnosis yet. He folded the prescription for the sleep aid Dr. Estrada had given him and stuffed it in his pocket. She'd assured him that the drug would knock him out cold at night—no chance for sleepwalking.

He planned to test it out tonight. Of course, if he was out cold and someone threatened the house or its occupants, how could he be any help to Devon and Michael? He'd have to figure it out.

"So we'll try the hypnosis next time?" He shook hands with Dr. Estrada.

"Yes. That should really help your memories come back, since they seem to be slipping through bit by bit already." She opened the door of her office and a piece of paper floated to the floor.

Kieran crouched down to retrieve it for her and on his way up, he peered into the empty waiting room. His heart thumped against his ribs as he handed the paper to Dr. Estrada.

She glanced at him over the top edge of the paper. "This is for you."

He snatched the paper from her hands, and then crumpled it in his fist. Why would she go out? He closed his eyes and dragged in a breath. It was daytime and she was on her way to meet a homicide detective. He couldn't stay chained to her side.

"Do you know where this alley is?"

"It cuts through Main Street to the park, behind the police station. When you get out to Main Street, hang a left and it's the second alley on your right. It's more like a little through-way than an alley."

He thanked her for the session and despite himself, jogged down the stairs to the sidewalk. He noticed Devon's car still parked on the street, so she must've walked.

Once on Main Street, he weaved between the tourists window shopping. He saw the sign for Vinnie's Pizza and cut down the street before it. Then he ran to the entrance of the alley. Panting, he stuttered to a stop and surveyed the alley.

A small van trundled toward him, a few surfboards strapped to the roof. A couple of boys careened past on skateboards and jumped over the cement steps behind a business.

His chest heaved and his breathing slowed. He located the red and white awning for Vinnie's. He waved. "Devon!"

Two faces turned toward him, and then his hand froze in the air and his blood ran cold.

Chapter Twelve

Kieran's gaze darted to the roof above Devon's head. Stacks of red roofing tiles shifted. Piles of bricks inched toward the rain gutters. Before he could process the implications, Kieran's feet began moving, his legs pumping. He called Devon's name again, the sound a roar in his ears.

His sprint caused his lungs to burn, and he couldn't manage more than a strangled cry from his throat. Devon's eyes widened at his approach. As the quarterback in high school and college, he'd had to execute a few tackles. Time to put one in play.

The muscles in his legs bunched as he sprang forward, his arms wide. He led with his chest, connecting with Devon's mid-section and Michael's leg dangling against her body. He wrapped his arms around both of them to cushion the impact of the fall.

All three of them hit the ground, and the backs of Kieran's hands scraped along the asphalt as he cradled Devon's head. Michael, sandwiched between them, grunted when Kieran's body crushed him against Devon's chest.

A crash resounded behind them, and bricks and tiles pelted Kieran's legs. Still covering Devon and Michael with his body, he twisted his head around and coughed at the red dust rising from a pile of debris that had destroyed the awning—the awning where Devon had stood with Michael seconds before.

Devon moaned and Michael whimpered. Kieran rolled from their bodies and sat on his heels. "Are you hurt anywhere?"

"What happened?" Devon pushed up to her elbows, and her jaw dropped when she saw the bricks and tiles scattered in the alley.

"Whoa." Michael sat up on Devon's stomach and she winced.

Kieran scooped him off and ran his hands from the boy's shoulders down his arms. "Are you okay, Michael? Does anything hurt?"

"My nose."

Kieran planted his finger on the tip of Michael's nose. "Must've squished it, but you look the same."

"H-how did you know those bricks and tiles were going to fall?"

Kieran gazed at the roof. Whoever shoved those

building materials over the edge was long gone now. Maybe someone saw him leaving the roof.

As Michael bent over to brush off his knees, Kieran met Devon's eyes and put a finger to his lips. "A premonition."

Her face white, Devon struggled to her feet and clamped Michael against her legs where he squirmed out of her grasp.

Kieran rose, shaking dust from his hair. "Where's Detective Marquette?"

"I—I don't know. Maybe still at the police station." She waved her arm at the back of a stucco building across the alley.

"What did he say when he called you?" Kieran knelt in front of Michael and checked out a small scrape on his elbow.

"He didn't call me. He texted me."

"He texted you?" Kieran's gut twisted. "How did you know it was Marquette?"

With trembling hands, she pulled her cell phone out of her purse. "I saved his number. His ID popped up when I got the text."

"Did you call him back?"

"He was in a meeting. I assumed that's why he texted me."

"What's he still doing in town?" Michael's small frame stiffened beneath his hands, so Kieran softened his tone. "What did the text say?"

Devon slid open her phone and held it in front

of him, cupping the screen. He read the message, and the knots in his belly got tighter.

"Where is he then?" He spread his arms to encompass the alley.

A few shopkeepers had wandered out their back doors and were pointing at the debris. The manager of Vinnie's was pawing through the pieces of his broken awning.

Devon shook her head. "I don't know where he is. He must still be in his meeting."

"Why would you leave Elena's office like that? You know you're in dan…" He trailed off as he picked a bit of dirt from Michael's hair. Michael didn't need to keep hearing how much danger surrounded his mom.

"I was going to meet a cop, for goodness' sakes…in a well-traveled alley behind the police station."

"Didn't do you much good." Kieran pointed to the roof of the building.

"We don't know anything yet, Kieran."

"That's right, but we're going to find out."

"Did you see what happened out here?" The manager of Vinnie's waved a piece of the tattered red-and-white-striped awning back and forth.

"The bricks and tiles fell from the roof, or someone pushed them off. Did you see anyone up there?"

The manager's face reddened. "If I find out it's

those damned teenagers who hang out back here, I'm going straight to the mayor."

"How would someone get off the roof?"

"It's not that high. You'd be surprised what those kids can do—jump onto Dumpsters, shimmy down trees. We even had some teens taking their skateboards up there and jumping from building to building." He shook a fist at the skateboarders who'd stopped doing tricks long enough to gawk at the mess of bricks on the ground. "If I find out you boys had anything to do with this, I'm going to get Mayor Davis to ban you kids from this alley."

The boys smirked and took off on their boards.

"How come no workers are up there working on the roof and facade?"

"There's some money dispute among the businesses. The city's paying for it, but some businesses think they're more deserving than others."

Devon tugged on Kieran's hand. "I'm calling Detective Marquette."

She punched in his number but got his voice mail. Then she pointed to the back of the police station. "Let's find him."

Kieran pinned the pizza manager with his gaze. "While you're at it, you tell the mayor that those falling bricks and tiles almost landed on a woman and a child."

My woman and child.

They crossed the alley together, only to find the

back door of the police station locked. Devon led him down a walkway to the front of the building.

Kieran held open the door for her as she marched to the front desk like she owned the place. She planted her hands on the counter. "Where is Detective Marquette?"

The officer's eyes popped. "You mean that homicide detective from SFPD who was meeting with the chief?"

"That's the one."

"He's not here."

"Do you mean the meeting's over and he already left?"

"Uh." The officer passed a hand over his mouth. "Yeah. He left after the meeting yesterday."

Kieran's hands clenched into fists, as he moved next to Devon, his shoulder touching hers.

"H-he didn't have a meeting with the chief today?"

"Not unless it was a teleconference. The chief's been holed up with the mayor for the past half hour."

Devon's shoulders slumped. "Maybe he was on the phone with Detective Marquette before his meeting with the mayor. Can I talk to the chief?"

"Hold on." The officer punched a button on the phone and spoke into the speaker. "Chief, Devon Reese is here to see you."

"Damn these Reeses. Are they ever going to leave this building?"

The officer closed his eyes. "Ah, Chief, you're on speaker phone."

"Send her back."

"Sorry, Ms. Reese." He looked both ways and hunched forward. "For the record, we're all looking forward to the day when your brother takes over as chief."

Devon grinned. "I appreciate that."

"And I second that emotion." A petite, fluffy woman scurried from the back and gave Devon a quick hug and patted Michael's head. "You're so big, Michael."

"Kieran, you remember Lucinda Lotts, don't you? My father's secretary."

That session with Dr. Estrada had helped, but not enough that he could immediately place every name and face in Coral Cove. "Of course I do."

"Good to have you home, Kieran." She crooked her finger at Michael. "Do you want to have a treat in my cubicle while your mom talks to Chief Evans, Michael?"

Devon mouthed the words "thank you" over Michael's head, but Kieran held his breath. Would Michael go with her?

Michael looked up at Devon for approval and she nodded. "He already had candy, Lucinda."

"Oh, we'll find something better than that." She

took his hand and led him to the back room divided by several cubicles.

Devon blew out a breath and squared her shoulders. "I'm ready."

Kieran placed his hand on the small of her back and steered her down the hallway. "Don't expect a warm welcome."

He rapped on the chief's door with a single knuckle.

"Come on in."

The chief swung his feet off the desk when they walked in, and the mayor hid a smile behind a cough.

"Sorry about that, Devon. It's been a tough day."

"Tell me about it." She blew a strand of hair from her face. "Did you have a meeting with Detective Marquette today?"

The chief shot a glance at the mayor. "No. He left yesterday. Didn't you talk to him?"

Kieran gritted his teeth. This sounded bad.

"I—I did see him…yesterday." Devon gripped the edge of the desk, her knuckles turning white.

Kieran draped his arm across her shoulder and he pressed her into the chair stationed behind her. She folded.

"What's this about?" Chief Evans sat forward in his seat.

Kieran wedged a hip against the corner of the desk. "Devon got a message from Detective Marquette earlier, asking her to meet him in the alley after his meeting with you."

The chief spread his hands. "Maybe it was an old message. I haven't heard from the detective since…" He scrabbled through some papers in his inbox. Then he punched a button on his phone. "Officer Dickens, didn't I get some message from Detective Marquette SFPD Homicide this morning?"

"Yes, sir."

"Do you have it?"

"It's out here, sir."

Chief Evans rolled his eyes. "Then bring it in here."

Devon held out her phone to the chief. "It's not an old message. You can see the time, eleven-forty today."

The chief squinted at the display. "Doesn't say the meeting is with me specifically, but I guess I'd know if one of my officers was meeting with him. Don't know why one of my officers would be meeting with him."

Officer Dickens poked his head into the room, a piece of pink paper from a message pad clutched in his hand. "I have it."

The chief held out his hand, his fingers wiggling. "Hand it over."

The officer held it out, and the chief snatched it

from his fingers. He perused the note with a wrinkled brow and then slapped it in front of Devon.

She hunched forward to read it, and then dropped her forehead onto the note.

A muscle in Kieran's jaw jumped and he rubbed a circle on Devon's back. "What is it? What does the note say, Devon?"

She raised her glassy eyes to his face and swallowed. "Detective Marquette lost his cell phone... Yesterday."

DEVON FELT LIKE SHE was drowning and her breath came out in little spurts. Her cell phone, in the middle of Chief Evans's desk, seemed to be emitting some sort of toxic vibe now.

How had the killer gotten Detective Marquette's cell phone? From there it would've been easy for him to text her since Detective Marquette probably had her number stored in his phone. The detective had called her several times since the murder.

Kieran's low, steady voice cleared the fog in her head.

"...so it's obvious, the person who's been stalking Devon stole Detective Marquette's phone and used it to lure Devon into that alley."

"Why would you agree to meet someone in an alley based on a text message?"

Devon's palm itched to smack the chief's fake incredulous look from his face. "It wasn't just someone. It was Detective Marquette. Why would I have any reason to believe the detective wasn't the one sending texts from his own phone?"

She pushed up from the chair, her fingernails curling into the blotter on the desk. "And it wasn't just some alley. It was the alley behind the police station, for God's sake. Why would I have any reason to believe I wouldn't be safe right behind the Coral Cove Police Station?" She smacked her forehead with the heel of her hand. "Oh, I know... because you're the chief."

Kieran ran his fingers down her arm, and she resisted an urge to shake him off.

"Devon..."

Her blood thumped in her temples and she pounded her fist on the desk, making the chief's favorite pen bounce. "I was eager to talk to Detective Marquette because you guys haven't done anything. Someone's trying to kill me because he or they have the mistaken idea I know something about Mrs. Del Vecchio's murder. And you're not doing anything to protect me. If Kieran weren't here, I'd be dead already."

"Our force isn't big enough..."

She snatched the pen off the desk and threw it across the room. Tyler ducked.

"Not only do you lead a worthless force, your officers are running around stealing."

"What are you talking about?" The chief remained seated, his hands folded on his desk.

"The night someone took a shot at me at Columbella House, Kieran and I had found a diary. When we went back for it, it was gone."

The chief's brows shot up. "Why would one of my men want to steal a diary?"

Devon waved her arms around and Tyler ducked again. "I don't know. It's just a general…a general…lack of direction in this department."

"Well, I'm sure things will be so much better when another Reese takes over this position." The chief managed a tight smile. "In the meantime, I'll have an officer start questioning the businesses in the area to see if anyone noticed someone going up or coming down from those rooftops."

Tyler cleared his throat. "And I'll certainly see about having the construction company secure its materials until building can resume."

"Yeah, and you might also want to recover that diary, Mayor Davis, since it could've belonged to your former fiancée. You know—the one who dumped you for her sister's boyfriend?"

She charged out of the room and stormed down the hallway to collect Michael from Lucinda. When she stumbled into the sunshine, Kieran gripping her hand, her pulse began to resume its normal beat.

"Wow." Kieran raised one eyebrow and his

mouth quirked at the corner. "You left with both barrels blazing. By the look on the mayor's face, he didn't know what hit him."

She scooped in a breath and blew it out with a sigh. "Chief Evans gets under my skin. Did you hear him? He was implying it was my fault someone almost dumped a ton of bricks on me."

"Look." Kieran placed a steadying hand on her shoulder. "It's not your fault, but don't go running around town without me, even in broad daylight, even when you think you're going to meet a cop. Not a good idea right now."

"I need to call Detective Marquette and tell him that someone used his cell to contact me, to set me up."

"Yeah, we'll do that, but first," he scooped up Michael and threw him over one shoulder, "we need to eat lunch."

Michael giggled and then shouted, "Pizza!"

Devon's nose tingled as she watched Kieran bounce Michael over his shoulder. Michael had actually giggled…and shouted, and both were like a sweet melody to her ears. She had no doubt Elena's sessions were helping Michael, but having a father, especially a father like Kieran—protective, strong—was having an even greater effect.

She made sure to lead them around to the front of Vinnie's so Michael wouldn't connect the collapsed awning with the pizza. After they ordered and ate a few slices, Michael pointed to a table where two boys had cars zooming across the tabletop.

"He can join them if he wants." The boys' mother smiled. "They have more cars."

Michael turned toward Devon, his eyes shining. It had been a while since he'd played with his friends from daycare. He hadn't been interested. She shooed him with her fingers. "Go ahead, but stay at their table where I can see you."

She and Kieran watched him dig two cars out of the boys' backpack and roll them around the pizza tins.

Kieran stretched out his legs and folded his arms behind his head. "Good sign, huh?"

"Lots of good signs since he's been here, despite the bathroom blowing up and those bricks almost falling on us."

"You'd think the threats to you here would drive him even further into his shell, but that's not happening. Elena must know what she's doing."

"Elena and you."

"Me?"

"Both times, Kieran, at the bathroom and in the alley, you were there to save us. That means a lot to Michael. I've done my best to protect him, but having a dad to keep you safe is different from having a mom around."

He dropped his chin to his chest and a smile

tugged at one side of his mouth as he watched Michael. "Been good for me, too."

"Speaking of which," she picked a piece of pepperoni from the pizza and popped it into her mouth, "how did your session with Elena go?"

"It was good." He patted his pocket. "She gave me a prescription for a sleeping aid and assured me I wouldn't be doing any sleepwalking if I took it."

"Or dreaming?"

"She couldn't guarantee that."

She wiped her fingers on a napkin and waved at Michael. "Well, at least that's good about the sleepwalking."

"Not necessarily."

"What do you mean?" She shredded the napkin without meeting his eyes. Was he looking for excuses not to spend the night with her?

"If I'm sound asleep, how am I going to protect you and Michael?"

She dropped the pieces of napkin on her plate and brushed her hands together. "I don't think these guys are going to be coming around the house. They have to know by now you're my personal bodyguard, and they're not going to know you're in slumber land instead of sitting by the window with your gun locked and loaded."

"Which is exactly where I should be."

Devon knew exactly where he should be—locked, loaded and in her bed.

"And what about your family?" Devon folded her arms and hunched her shoulders, ready to do battle. "Was Dr. Estrada able to convince you to call your parents and Colin to let them know you're alive? You talk about protection—you have to put Colin out of his misery."

Kieran traced a bead of moisture on the outside of his glass with his fingertip. "I'm going to call them...as soon as this mess is over. As soon as you and Michael are safe. Before I see Colin again, it's important to make sure he knows he doesn't have to take care of me, or worry about me."

"So you want to prove you can take care of business on your own first." The man had a mountain of stubborn pride, but he had a point. "I get it."

"Good." He skewered her with one dark eye. "I need to call my family in my own time."

"So let's get this over with." She unhooked her purse from the back of her chair and fished for her cell phone in the side pocket. "I'm going to call Detective Marquette in case Chief Evans couldn't be bothered."

"Good idea." Kieran wandered toward the table where Michael was playing and crouched beside him.

Devon blinked. If she was going to get teary-eyed every time she saw Kieran with Michael, she'd better invest in some waterproof mascara. Sighing, she punched in the number for the SFPD Homicide Division and got a receptionist. "Could you page Detective Marquette, please? This is really important."

Several minutes later, her cell phone rang and she waved it at Kieran. The display showed a restricted number.

Kieran swooped back to the table and held out his hand, palm up. "Let me get it. The killer has your number."

His words sent a line of fear trickling down her spine, and she dropped the phone into his hand.

"Hello?"

She held her breath and crumpled her pizza-stained napkin.

"Yeah, this is Roarke." He nodded at her. "I'll let Devon tell you the story."

He handed the phone back to her. "Detective Marquette? This is Devon Reese. I got a text message from your cell phone."

She told him about the text and the meeting request and the near miss in the alley. He punctuated her narrative with grunts, curses and whistles.

When she finished, he cursed again. "That SOB must've stolen my cell phone while I was in Coral Cove."

Her heart rate accelerated. "Do you have any idea where it was stolen? Did you talk to someone suspicious here? Did anyone initiate a conversation with you?"

"Whoa. Who's the detective here? I guess he played me for a fool because I honestly believed I left it somewhere in Coral Cove. That's why I called the chief—thought I might've left it at the station."

"And he didn't even bother to call you back."

Marquette ignored her jab at a fellow officer of the law. "This guy really wants at you. Whoever he is."

"You don't really think it has anything to do with my brother's undercover work, do you?"

"It's still a possibility, Ms. Reese. Tell you what. I need you up here in the city anyway to look at some mug shots of Johnny Del's former cohorts."

"You can't just scan them and send them to my email?"

"Not allowed to do that. You have to physically sign off on them. Besides, coming back here might be a good idea. Get you out of danger's way, or better yet, if the creep follows you we might finally get a line on him."

She hunched her shoulders. Why did everyone have to keep reminding her of the danger she faced? "I'm not sure, Detective. I don't want to bring my son back there right now."

"Think about it. I need you to look at these six-packs. Who knows? You might even recognize one of the men."

When she ended the call, she slumped back in her seat. "He wants me to go to the city to look at some mug shots of Johnny Del's partners."

"He mentioned that before. What's the problem?"

Her gaze darted toward Michael trading cars with the other boys at the table. "I hadn't planned on taking Michael back to San Francisco just yet."

"He should be okay if you don't take him back to your place where Granny Del was murdered."

"A-and you'll be with us?"

He planted his hands on the table and leaned forward. "I'm not letting you out of my sight."

LATER THAT EVENING, KIERAN watched Devon put the finishing touches on the root beer floats as Michael jabbed his fingers into the vanilla ice cream. That was normal behavior for a four-year-old boy, right?

Michael seemed a lot less tense now than he did when Kieran had first plucked him off those rocks a few days ago. He shifted his gaze back to the baseball game where the camera panned the crowd, zeroing in on a father and son. They mugged for the camera and the dad tugged at the boy's Giants baseball cap.

The man made it seem so effortless…this being-a-father business. Kieran wanted lessons, a play-book, a different life. What did that man on the TV screen know of brutality, of torture, of survival? And why couldn't Kieran erase *those* memories from his fragmented mind? Experiences not conducive to being a father...or a husband.

A small hand tapped his shoulder. "Root beer floats."

"Thanks, Michael." He tugged on his ear. "I hope you put a lot of ice cream in there."

"With my own two hands." Michael splayed a pair of freshly scrubbed hands in front of him.

"Mmm." Kieran raised his brows at Devon.

"Trust me. He used an ice cream scooper."

Kieran gripped the handle of the frosty mug and tipped the root beer into his mouth through the sweet foam. "Perfect."

They slurped through their desserts, and Kieran collected the empty mugs and brought them to the kitchen sink. He rinsed the mugs and squirted a stream of yellow dishwashing liquid into the warm water to wash the remaining pans from dinner. He called over his shoulder. "Are we going to spend the night in the city or go up and back in one day?"

"Uh, I'm not sure. We're not going to stay at my apartment. Maybe we should get a hotel room... or two, so we have a home base in case Detective Marquette keeps us waiting."

"When you called him back, did he give you a specific time?"

"He said around two o'clock, but he's in court that day and isn't sure he'll be finished by then."

"We can always take a long, late lunch if he isn't."

"Let's play it by ear."

He grabbed a dish towel and wiped his hands. When he turned toward the living room, he tripped to a stop. He took a deep breath and sauntered toward Michael's stiff frame, facing away from the TV.

When Kieran had gone into the kitchen, Michael had been watching the game, sitting cross-legged with his knees bouncing. Now he'd drawn up his knees to his chest and wrapped his arms around his legs.

Kieran shot a glance at Devon, who shrugged, lines of worry creasing her forehead.

Kieran plopped on the floor next to Michael. "Do you want to watch the rest of the game?"

Michael burrowed his chin into his knees.

"Someday I'll take you to see a live baseball game in San Francisco. Would you like that?"

Michael pulled his arms up to his knees, hiding his face.

Kieran's hand hovered at the back of Michael's head. Should he touch him? Leave him alone? What would the dad at the baseball game do?

Kieran dropped his hand. "If you're worried about going back home tomorrow, it's okay. It's okay to be worried, but we're not going to your apartment and I'll be with you."

Michael rocked back and forth, and Devon jumped up from the couch. "We'll be at the police station most of the time, Michael. It'll be fine, and we can have lunch on Fisherman's Wharf."

She ruffled Michael's hair as she wrinkled her nose at Kieran. "Time for bed."

Kieran went with her to tuck Michael in, but any progress they'd made in the past few days had evaporated. Michael had withdrawn, his voice silent once again.

Kieran listened to the story Devon read aloud, and he contributed sound effects and silly comments but Michael wasn't biting.

Once Michael dozed off, they retreated to the living room.

Devon collapsed on the couch and curled her legs beneath her. "Ugh. Maybe we should've discussed the trip privately and then just sprung it on him tomorrow in the car."

"I don't think that would've been a good idea. In fact, I mishandled it completely by mentioning the trip in the kitchen. He's a bright kid. Why wouldn't he pick up on what I was saying? We should've told him first."

"Okay, don't beat yourself up. Sometimes it's

not easy to figure out the best way to go. If we had sat down with him and told him we were going back to San Francisco, maybe that would have signaled to him that we were worried about it. By discussing it casually, he might approach it casually."

"But he didn't."

"Parents can't know everything." She bit her lip as she sent a worried look at the hallway. "I'm sure he'll be fine tomorrow."

They switched from the game to a movie, and Kieran traced the edge of the sleeping pill bottle in his pocket with the tip of his finger. A couple of those and he'd be knocked out for the night— no nightmares, no memories, no sleepwalking. No Devon.

She curled up beside him on the couch, her head propped up on the arm and her toes inches from his thigh. Her smooth calves curved up from slender ankles.

His fingers inched toward her skin for just a small taste. He ran the pad of his thumb along her silky flesh and her leg twitched. He circled a spot around a light freckle and her toes curled into his thigh.

Encircling her ankles with his fingers, he drew her feet onto his lap. "You can stretch out."

She sighed and wiggled her toes. Her hair fanned out across her chest, and he swore he could see the golden strands tremble with each beat of her heart.

His own heart thudded against his ribcage. When she dug her heels into the inside of his thigh, a rush of potent desire flooded his senses.

He cupped the heel of her foot in his hand and raised it to his lips. He pressed a kiss against the bone on the top of her foot, and she sucked in a breath.

Her other foot crept close to his crotch where she tucked it between his legs. He gritted his teeth to suppress the groan that had clawed its way up from his gut. When the wave of need subsided into a dull ache, he pulled in a breath between clenched teeth. "You have very talented feet."

Something between a snort and a giggle bubbled from her lips and she wiggled the foot he still held captive. "You ain't seen nothin' yet. There's magic in these toes."

He took her big toe between his teeth. "I'd prefer it if you used other parts of your anatomy."

"And I'd prefer it if you used other parts of yours." Her gaze dropped to his lap where his erection was straining against the fly of his shorts.

He took one of her legs and tucked it on his left side and then rolled to his stomach, facing her on the couch. She needed no encouragement. She wrapped both of her legs around his waist and he lowered his body to press against hers.

The smell of her engulfed him, wildflowers and sunshine and musky woman, drawing him into an orbit of heady passion. A place where the mind didn't matter, where the heightened sensitivities of the body held sway.

He took possession of her lips. He plundered her mouth like a man too long without water, without nectar, without sustenance. His pelvis grinded against hers, seeking a release for his body that he had to hold in check.

She arched against him, slipping a hand between their sealed bodies to unbutton her blouse. When it gaped open, Kieran ran his tongue down her throat to the sweet spot between her breasts. He slipped one hand inside her bra and caressed her while he circled his thumb around her nipple, bringing it to a ripe peak.

Bending his head, he replaced his thumb with the tip of his tongue, teasing her until she cried out.

She reached for his fly and yanked at the buttons, almost ripping them from his shorts. She flattened her hands against his belly and then slid them inside his boxers. Her hands fondled the length of his erection, and he closed his eyes, dragging a shuddering breath into his lungs.

Where had all his self-control gone?

Maybe if he could get Devon to move her hands to another part of his body, he could rein in his runaway lust. She skimmed her fingernails along his tight flesh, and he thrust forward, a growl rumbling in his chest.

Balancing on one forearm, he grabbed both of her wrists and pulled her hands away from the danger zone. She had the nerve to smirk in his face. *She'd pay for that.*

He rose to his knees, straddling her. He tugged at the button on her pants, and yanked them down by the zipper.

"Hey, you're going to rip them." She slapped at his hand and lifted her hips from the couch, bringing her parts dangerously close to his parts.

She hitched up on her elbows and shimmied out of the pants, which caused another sledgehammer of need to pound into his belly.

He grabbed her hips, his fingers digging into her soft, rounded flesh. Then he scooted back until his head was level with the juncture of her legs.

"Oh." Her eyes widened for a moment before her lids fluttered to half-mast, and she weaved her fingers through his hair, tugging him forward.

He tasted her, and with a soft moan, she dug her nails into his scalp. He caressed her swollen flesh with his tongue, and the taste and feel of her acted like a drug coursing through his veins.

He didn't want a sleeping pill to knock him out. He'd rather stay awake all night long making love to Devon. He wanted to relearn every curve and hollow of her body. He drew back and landed a line of kisses along her inner thigh.

She gasped and clutched at his shoulder. "More, Kieran. I've missed you so much. I want all of you."

Could he deliver? He'd gladly offer her all of his body, but could he ever let her into the dark recesses of his mind?

He'd start with his body.

He swung his legs over the side of the couch to peel off his shorts as Devon unhooked her bra and shrugged off her blouse.

They needed to finish this in the bedroom, or start it all over again. Kieran stepped out of his shorts and scooped up Devon from the couch.

And then he almost dropped her as a shrill scream sliced through the house.

Chapter Thirteen

Devon squirmed in Kieran's arms. She knew that sound and it pierced a hole in her heart.

Kieran had tightened his hold on her in an instinctive response to the scream, but she didn't need his protection now. Michael did.

"It's Michael." She forced the words from her constricted lungs.

Kieran released her and grabbed his shorts while she stuffed her arms into her blouse and clawed at the floor for her panties.

She banged her shin on the coffee table as she barreled toward Michael's room. She shoved at the door, which she had left ajar and flicked on the light. Michael always recovered better from one of his nightmares with the lights on.

She stumbled to a stop and pressed her fist against her mouth.

Michael was sitting up in his bed, his rigid back lined up against the headboard, his wide eyes staring, unseeing.

Kieran nudged her. "Wake him up. He's still sleeping."

She tiptoed to the bed and sank onto the mattress. Brushing a dark lock of hair from his pale face, she whispered, "Michael, it's okay. Wake up now."

Kieran hovered behind her, his breath harsh. "Wake him up, Devon."

Michael's jaw tensed and his eyes flicked from side to side. She'd never seen him like this before. Once he screamed, he woke up from his nightmare. Now he seemed trapped in another world experiencing private horrors.

Kieran reached around her and grabbed Michael's shoulders. He gave him a shake and shouted. "Wake up, Michael. Wake up." He ripped the covers from Michael's clenched fists, and shouted again.

Michael blinked. His body bucked. His mouth began working and mewing sounds escaped from his lips.

Devon lurched forward and folded her arms around him. Stroking his hair, she murmured in his ear.

He mumbled something into her shoulder.

"It's okay now, Michael. You're safe."

He twisted his head to the side. "I'm not going home, I'm not going home, I'm not going home."

Devon glanced at Kieran and shook her head.

"That's fine. You don't have to go home. Do you want another story?"

Devon read him another story with more sound effects from Kieran. Every few pages, Michael would interrupt the story and ask if he was going home tomorrow. And every time, Devon assured him he was not.

When he drifted off to sleep, she and Kieran slipped out of the room. With tears blurring her vision, Devon went to her bedroom and flung herself across the bed.

"I thought he was getting better. That's the worst I've seen him."

"Have you tried asking him about his nightmares?"

She nodded. "I've tried, but he claims he doesn't remember them."

Kieran sat next to her and rubbed her back. "It was just a nightmare and he couldn't wake up. He'll be fine."

"You don't think that will cause a setback or anything, do you?"

"Nah. He's just not ready to go home."

She swiped a tear from her cheek. Even if Kieran was here to help carry the burden, she still had to remain strong for Michael.

"D-do you think you can stay here with him while I go up north to meet with Detective Marquette?"

"No way. I'm not letting you go to the city by yourself. Can you leave Michael here while we go up? You must still have some friends in Coral Cove."

"I do, but none of them really knows Michael. I'm afraid he wouldn't stay with a stranger."

"How about Dr. Estrada? She's not a stranger. He likes her, trusts her."

"I don't know if he'll stay with anyone but me right now…except maybe you."

"We'll drive up and back, no staying overnight. Besides, you make dangerous company right now."

She covered her eyes with her forearm. Was being with her putting Michael in danger? He'd been with her in the bathroom and in the alley. The thug who killed Mrs. Del Vecchio obviously didn't have a problem with collateral damage.

"I suppose we can try it, but if he freaks out again Detective Marquette will just have to show me those pictures another day."

"The sooner you look at that six-pack, the better. Who knows? You might be able to ID someone who's been hanging around Coral Cove, and then Marquette can end this thing."

She rolled to her side and propped her head up with her hand, her elbow digging into the bed. I'm glad you're here, Kieran. I don't know how I would've faced this chaos without you."

He dabbed at a tear still hanging on the end of

her lashes. "The way you've always faced it—with courage and fearlessness and gumption."

"Did you just say 'gumption'?" She raised an eyebrow. "How do you know about my gumption? You haven't been around to see it."

"I see it now. I see it in our son."

With her free hand, she reached forward and slid her finger beneath the string that held his eye patch to his head. She slipped the patch from his face and tossed it to the floor. His eye twitched, but his body remained still. She smoothed her fingers across the puckered skin surrounding his eye.

Then she cupped his jaw, the bristles of his beard tickling her palm. She'd wanted him before Michael's nightmare, and she wanted him even more now. Maybe Michael's scream had doused the fire and passion they'd shared on the couch, but now she needed something else from him. Could he give it to her? He was convinced he couldn't. She'd seen it in his face, in the way he pulled away from her.

He turned his head to kiss the center of her palm. Stretching out on the bed next to her, he pulled her close and she felt his heartbeat reverberate in his chest as she laid her cheek against his flesh, crisscrossed with scars from another place and time.

The blouse she'd pulled on in haste hiked up to

her hips, and Kieran slid his hands beneath her panties and peeled them from her body.

While he removed his shorts, she unbuttoned the top two buttons of her blouse and pulled it over her head. Lying naked beside Kieran, Devon closed her eyes awaiting another assault from his hands, mouth, tongue.

His calloused fingers traced a line from under her arm to the bottom of her hip. His soft lips planted a kiss on her collarbone, his tongue testing her flesh.

He transferred his kiss to her lips, and the warmth of his mouth against hers melted her bones. He continued his slow exploration of her body with his strong hands, hands that had inflicted injury, pain and death.

Now they expressed only love.

He nudged her onto her back and pressed his body, full-length, against hers. His warm flesh electrified her skin and she gasped in the sheer pleasure of the sensation.

"Did I hurt you?" He pushed up onto his forearms, and she immediately felt the loss of him.

Stroking his back and buttocks, she whispered, "Absolutely not. Never. Come back to me."

He lowered himself again, sealing himself to her so there was no distinction between where the lines of his body left off and hers began. He kissed her mouth and then nibbled her earlobe. "I love you. I never stopped loving you."

A sob escaped her lips, and she trailed a finger around his eye. "I want you, Kieran. I need you to make me feel whole again."

He slipped one leg between hers and then eased inside her. His body shuddered once and then the tenderness ended. He drove into her core over and over while she moaned and sighed and asked for more.

His muscles were hard and tense beneath her kneading hands as he restrained himself, held back. Then she exploded and shattered into a million pieces, giving him his cue.

With a guttural cry, he let go. And in the midst of his own pleasure he sought her mouth again, his kisses hard and hot. And then she knew.

Kieran Roarke had finally come home to her.

DEVON DROPPED A KISS on top of her son's silky hair, so much like his father's.

"Tell Kier…your dad to hurry up." When Michael disappeared down the hallway, she turned to Elena. "I really appreciate this, Elena."

"Absolutely my pleasure. Michael and I can use the time to get better acquainted outside of the office."

"I hope it's not too much of an inconvenience."

"Not at all. Like I told you on the phone this

morning, I had only two patients today and one of them always cancels on me."

"Thank you. We won't be gone long. Should be back for dinner."

"If it's okay with you, we'll go on a picnic at the beach. We won't go to a swimming beach, so Michael won't be in the water."

"That's fine. Just call or text me if there's a problem."

Kieran emerged from brushing his teeth in the bathroom, carrying Michael on his shoulders. "All the details settled?"

Devon smiled. Michael looked so comfortable up there, and after the night she and Kieran had spent in her bed maybe Kieran would realize they belonged together as a family. "I'm ready to go. Elena has a fun day planned with Michael. Is Sam joining you today?"

A pink tint touched Elena's cheeks. "No. He had to go out of town today."

Reaching up to tickle Michael's cheek, Devon said, "Have fun today. We'll be back for dinner."

"Don't go home, Mommy."

Devon's smile froze on her lips. Her son shouldn't have to worry like this. "I'm not going home, sweet pea. Just going to see a policeman, like Uncle Dylan."

"I'll keep Mommy safe." Kieran hoisted Michael off his shoulders and placed him on his feet.

After several hugs and kisses, Devon pulled the car out of the driveway and hit the coast highway. Chewing her lip, Devon glanced into the rearview mirror. "Do you think Michael will be okay?"

"Elena will keep him safe. The guy's after you, not Michael."

"Yeah, I wonder if he knows I'm on my way back to the city to talk to the detective on the case. I wonder if he's following us right now."

"He can follow us right to the police station."

Three hours later, Devon steered the car across the cable car tracks on Powell and headed into the underground parking structure at the SFPD's central station. She'd called Detective Marquette from the road, and he'd assured her he'd be in his office and ready with the pictures.

She'd also called Elena, and she and Michael were packing for their beach picnic. Leaving Michael with Elena had been the right thing to do. No way could Michael have handled this trip to the police station.

Devon's gaze darted around the busy floor where the elevator had deposited them. This scene made *her* nervous.

"Are you okay?" Kieran's warm breath caressed her earlobe, and she straightened her shoulders.

"Yep. Let's get this over with. Maybe we'll get lucky."

They asked for Detective Marquette at the front

desk, and the officer paged him. A few minutes later, he came striding from the cluster of cubicles and offices in the back, hand outstretched. "Glad you could make it up. Sorry for the inconvenience. Some things we still have to do in person."

As the big man squeezed her hand in a powerful grip, Devon asked, "Any luck with your cell phone?"

"Nope. I've called it a few times, but it goes straight to voice mail. I've got an order in with my carrier to ping it, but I can pretty much already guess where it is—probably at the bottom of the ocean or in a Dumpster."

Kieran shook Marquette's hand. "Any idea where and how it was stolen?"

The detective lifted one suit-clad shoulder. "After I met with the chief, I did some shopping on the main drag for my wife. She loves that knick-knacky tourist stuff. Gets crowded in those shops and I usually keep my work phone in my jacket pocket. Would've been easy for a pickpocket to snatch it."

He jerked his thumb over his shoulder. "Let's have a look at those pictures. Most of Johnny Del's former partners are getting up there in age now, but who knows? Maybe you'll recognize some geezer from the streets of Coral Cove."

"I don't see how some senior citizen could be throwing Molotov cocktails around and running along rooftops." Devon shuffled after Detective Marquette, her hands in her pockets.

"I said they were getting up there, not knocking on death's door." He ushered them into a small room with a table, four chairs and a two-way window. A loose-leaf binder lay open on the table.

"Have a seat and let me tell you how this is going to work." Detective Marquette pulled out a chair for Devon and she perched on the edge.

Kieran sat next to her and flipped through the binder.

Detective Marquette tapped the first page encased in plastic. "Five sheets with six mug shots each. Members of Del Vecchio's gang of thieves, including Johnny Del himself, are scattered throughout. Have a look. Let me know if any of the faces jump out at you—people you may have seen around your apartment house. Someone you've seen on the streets of Coral Cove."

Taking a deep breath, Devon scooted the book closer to Kieran. "You can look at them, too."

She studied the photos, the lines and creases on each worn face telling stories, sketching personalities. The men in these pictures weren't hot off their first crimes or even the last crimes that had put them away. These mug shots of late middle-aged men full of regret and bitterness had obviously replaced the young criminals full of bravado and swagger.

When she turned to the fourth page, a pair of dark eyes challenged her, the twist of the lips knowing and seductive. She traced her finger around the face.

Kieran sucked in a breath. "Someone you know?"

"I'm not sure." She brought the book closer to her face and smoothed over the wavy plastic with the side of her thumb. "This one looks familiar."

"Let me see." Kieran took the book from her hands and zeroed in on the photo with his good eye. "Kind of looks like Sam."

"Sam? Elena's Sam?" She jerked the book out of his hands and squinted at the mug shot. "Too old."

"I didn't say it *was* Sam. Just looks a little like him around the eyes and mouth."

Detective Marquette cleared his throat. "Who's Sam?"

"Michael's seeing a therapist in Coral Cove, Elena Estrada. Sam Frost is her boyfriend."

"How old is Sam?" Marquette scribbled Sam's name on his notepad.

"He's about Elena's age—early fifties maybe? What do you think, Kieran?"

"Is that how old Elena is? At first I thought her new boyfriend was younger."

"Well, he's in good shape and I think he dyes his hair."

"Doesn't matter if the guy's her age or if she's

robbing the cradle, this man—" he tapped the photo "—Bud, The Pelican, Pelicano, died in prison last year."

"W-was he one of Johnny Del's cohorts?" Devon flipped to the next page to escape The Pelican's intense stare.

"Yes, he was."

Devon shivered and studied the six-pack on the following page.

Kieran scooted his chair back, stood up and stretched. He paced behind Detective Marquette and leaned over his left shoulder. Pointing to a thick folder on the table, he said, "Mind if I take a look?"

"Go ahead." The detective shoved the folder toward the edge of the table where Kieran scooped it up.

He flipped through the pages as Devon finished perusing the mug shots. She slapped the book closed. "Nothing. I don't recognize anyone there from my apartment house or from Coral Cove. If one of those guys did kill Granny Del and is now after me, he's keeping himself well hidden—and for no reason. I didn't see a thing."

"We've made it clear we have no witnesses, Ms. Reese."

Kieran dropped the open file folder on the table and jabbed his finger at the drawing of Granny Del's kitchen. "That's where she was found?"

Devon leaned over. "Yeah, in the kitchen. She must've been washing dishes or something. That's how the guy drowned her—dunked her head in the kitchen sink. By the time I showed up, the sink was overflowing."

"And what's this?" He scraped his fingernail around a rectangle penciled on the wall.

"That's an old dumbwaiter. We don't use it."

Tilting his head, Kieran massaged his temple above the eye patch. "You think the killer was trying to get information from Mrs. Del Vecchio, Detective?"

"Probably. Why else kill the old lady?" He smacked his fist on the book. "All these guys had already done their time. There was always a rumor that Johnny Del had stashed away some money from one of their heists. Someone probably came looking for it and tried to get it out of Johnny's widow."

"That's crazy. Mrs. Del Vecchio didn't have a lot of money."

Detective Marquette shrugged. "These rumors get passed around among family members until they become legend. Now I need you to sign a statement that you viewed the photos."

He slipped a piece of paper from the front of the binder and placed it in front of Devon. "Sign and date here and put your comments in the box."

"I guess I should put that number twenty-three,

The Pelican, looked like Sam, huh, Kieran?" She held the pen poised above the comments box on the form. Then she glanced at Kieran, still studying the crime scene drawing. "Kieran?"

"Huh?" He looked up, his brows drawn over his nose.

"Sam and The Pelican. Should I note the similarity?"

"Yeah. Detective Marquette?"

"Sure. Why not? I'll look at Pelicano more closely if you want."

Devon scribbled in the box and then shoved back from the table. "Let's get home. I'm going to text Elena first."

She pulled her cell from her purse and typed in a text message to Elena asking if everything was okay. A minute later, Elena responded with, *ok on picnic.*

"Ready, Kieran?"

He dropped the file folder on the table. "Let's go."

Kieran's eye ached, and he fumbled in his pocket for the small bottle of ibuprofen he kept there. They thanked Detective Marquette, who promised to keep Devon informed and suggested she find another place other than Coral Cove for R and R.

When they got in the car, Kieran popped the

pill in his mouth and gulped some warm water from the bottle in the cup holder.

"What's wrong?"

"My eye's throbbing."

"Is that why you were so distracted back there?"

"How far is your apartment from here?"

"Not far. I'm in North Beach. It's a few blocks north of here, up Columbus." She narrowed her eyes. "Why?"

"I'd like to have a look around."

"My place? We can't get into Granny Del's."

"Your place will do." He flattened the pad of his thumb against the two vertical lines between her eyebrows. No need to worry her about a hunch. "Since we're so close, I'd like to see where you and Michael live."

She started the engine and backed out of the parking slot. "Okay, but I promised Michael I wouldn't go home."

He covered her hand on the steering wheel. "And I promised him I'd take care of you."

It took less than five minutes to arrive at the front of Devon's apartment house—an old Victorian that had been converted. She parallel parked in a small space and reached across his knees for the glove compartment. She pulled out a plastic card and hung it from her rearview mirror. "Parking permit for the neighborhood."

He followed her up the three steps to the front

door and stood to the side while she inserted a key. So how'd the killer get in without anyone seeing him?

Kieran looked up. No security cameras.

Devon slipped through the front door and propped it open for him with the toe of her shoe. She pointed to a door to the left. "That's the infamous laundry room. If I hadn't decided to put a load in that day, I wouldn't be in this mess now."

"If you hadn't decided to put a load in that day, you never would've come back to Coral Cove and run into me." He grabbed her hand and kissed it.

She closed her fist around the material of his shirt and pulled him near. "You would've found me, Kieran. Wherever I was, you would've found me."

He pressed his lips against hers and then ducked around her to peek into the laundry room. "Your back was to the door when it slammed shut?"

"Absolutely. I thought it was the annoying teen who lives on my floor." She tugged at his arm. "This is Mrs. Del Vecchio's apartment."

Kieran tried the handle. No yellow tape crisscrossing the door, but it was locked. "You're right above her?"

"This way."

He followed her up the stairs and waited while she unlocked her door. Stepping through the door, he blinked. Sun soaked through every window in the place. Casual furniture and colorful prints on the walls didn't make the apartment look like some place you'd want to flee. "It suits you."

"It used to suit me. How am I ever going to get Michael back here?"

"When you're safe and this is all over, he'll heal." He took a turn around the room. "Is your layout the same as Mrs. Del Vecchio's?"

"Yeah, pretty much."

He wandered toward the kitchen, sudden apprehension clawing at his gut. He glanced at the sink, imagining it full of sudsy water and an old woman struggling for her life. He stopped short and gripped the edge of the tiled counter. "Is that the dumbwaiter?"

Devon came up behind him, clutching one of Michael's toys in her hand. "Yeah. If you couldn't tell, this was an old house. The builders left the dumbwaiter thinking it would give the place character, but it's been a pain."

"Why?"

She waved the toy at the dumbwaiter. "Because you can manipulate it from the inside and Michael kept crawling in there."

Cold fear slithered up his spine. "Does it work?"

"Yeah, it works."

"And it goes down to Mrs. Del Vecchio's kitchen."

She cocked her head. "Yes."

"Did Michael ever use it to go down to Granny Del's?"

"H-he did, but I told him to stop. I was afraid it would break or he'd get trapped." She hugged the toy. "Why the interest in the dumbwaiter, Kieran?"

He took two steps and slid open the door of the dumbwaiter. The space yawned in front of him, inviting, doubly so for a young boy. He toed off his running shoes and ducked inside.

"What are you doing?"

"I'm going in."

"Why? What's this about?" Devon's voice had raised two octaves. She'd caught his edge of worry. "You're not going to fit."

"I'll be right back." He folded his frame, pulled his knees up to his chest and crammed his body inside the cavity. He yanked at the ropes to lower the dumbwaiter, and it inched down the space inside the wall.

A four-year-old boy would love this.

When the dumbwaiter descended and plunked to a stop, Kieran slid open the door just a few inches. He had a view of Mrs. Del Vecchio's kitchen…and her sink.

Hand over hand, he pulled at the ropes, ascending back to Devon's apartment with his heart hammering in his chest. He slid the door open, and

Devon's face, etched with worry, appeared in front of him.

"What is it? What did you see?"

"Everything. Michael is the one who witnessed Granny Del's murder."

Chapter Fourteen

Devon sagged to the floor and Kieran scrambled from the dumbwaiter to catch her.

Her knees hit the tiles, and Kieran crouched beside her, his words drowned out by the roaring in her ears.

"No. No, that's impossible. He was sleeping."

"Think about it, Devon." He cupped her face with both of his hands. "Why would Michael be so upset that a neighbor died? Most kids his age don't even understand the concept of death."

"They were close. Sh-she…" Oh, God. Devon covered her eyes. Mrs. Del Vecchio was the one who had encouraged Michael to use the dumbwaiter to visit her. Had Michael defied her rule in favor of Granny Del's much more exciting one?

She repeated. "No. It can't be."

Kieran continued in his low voice, which seemed so odd next to the panic sweeping through her body. "The water in the sink. Do you remember how upset he was that day in the kitchen? Our arguing hadn't upset him. It was the overflowing sink—just like the overflowing sink in Mrs. Del Vecchio's kitchen when she was being murdered."

The truth of Kieran's words hammered at her consciousness. Trying to push it away, she grasped at straws. "I'm not saying it's true, but if it were, if Michael really did witness the murder, the killer doesn't know that. The killer's after me."

Please, God.

Kieran pulled her against his chest. "I don't think so, Devon."

Her body convulsively jerked in his arms, and he wrapped her tighter in his embrace.

"The shot at Columbella House. That was meant for me. Michael wasn't even there."

"Maybe the killer figured he could get to Michael better with you out of the way."

She struggled out of his arms and pummeled his chest. "Stop. It's not true."

"Devon." He grabbed her by the shoulders and shook her. "And now you're out of the way. We need to get back to Michael."

This new realization dropped on her head like an anvil and she gasped for breath. She scrambled to her feet and lunged for her purse on the table in the entryway. She punched in the number for Elena's cell phone and nearly cried out when she heard Elena's voice mail message.

She dragged in a breath and huffed it out.

"Elena, this is Devon. Michael is in danger. We think he's the one who witnessed the murder. Take him to the Coral Cove P.D. as soon as you get this message and call me back."

Kieran smoothed a hand down her back. "That's the way. He'll be fine once Elena gets him to the police station. We'll pick him up there and head out of town."

Another thought slammed against her brain and she sank to the nearest chair. "Kieran, why does Elena's new boyfriend look like one of Johnny Del's gang members?"

Kieran's face showed no surprise, only a deepening of the lines bracketing his mouth. "Coincidence. You heard Detective Marquette—The Pelican is dead."

"How did the killer know we were at Elena's office? How did he know when he texted me that you wouldn't be there? You know he never would've tried anything with you there."

A muscle twitched in Kieran's jaw and he rubbed it with his thumb. "I don't know, Devon."

She bent forward and leaned her forehead on her knees. "Sam came into Elena's waiting room that day, remember? He'd forgotten something. That told him Elena was seeing Michael first and you next. He knew I'd be waiting for you with Michael."

"What did Elena say this morning? Sam was out of town today."

"Yeah, out of town because he thought we were all going to San Francisco. What do you want to bet he changed his mind after he heard from Elena?"

"Let's get back." Kieran grabbed her hand and pulled her out of the chair.

When they got to the car, Devon called the Coral Cove P.D. "Clark, you need to look for Dr. Elena Estrada. My son is with her and he's in danger."

"From Dr. Estrada?"

Devon pounded the steering wheel. "No, from Sam...Sam Frost. He's the financial adviser who just moved into the same building as Dr. Estrada."

"I don't think the chief's going to launch a manhunt on your say-so, Devon. Is there some kind of APB out for Dr. Estrada or a warrant for this Sam?"

"No. I'm telling you. My son is in danger. Elena took him on a picnic to the beach."

"We have miles of beaches here, Devon."

"Start searching them!" she screamed into the phone and threw it against the dashboard.

Kieran scooped up the phone from the floor. "I'm calling Detective Marquette."

He left a message for the detective and then

placed the phone in the console. "Elena will protect Michael from Sam."

Devon shot a sideways glance at Kieran, his face dark and menacing. She'd put her money on Kieran over Elena, Chief Evans and the entire CCPD and SFPD wrapped together.

She maneuvered through the streets toward Fisherman's Wharf and then hit The Embarcadero. The tension in her shoulders didn't abate until she accelerated onto the freeway.

"Try Elena again."

Kieran shook his head as he held the phone to his ear. "Not picking up."

Devon said a silent prayer for the safety of her son as she raced up the freeway. *God, keep my son safe until his father can rescue him.*

DEVON BLEW INTO CORAL COVE and raced up the back way to the center of town. They planned to drop by her mom's house first and then check Elena's office before hitting the beaches.

Devon's stomach dropped when she didn't spot Elena's car out front. "She's not here."

"Let's check inside in case she left some indication where they were going."

"She texted me over three hours ago that they were picnicking at the beach. They wouldn't still be there. Look at the weather." She waved her arm at the overcast skies.

"Maybe she went to her office for something."

Devon glanced at her cell phone on the way back to the car. "Still no call from Detective Marquette."

"They're busy at those big city departments. Give him time."

She choked. "We don't have time, Kieran. We need the police out looking for this guy, and Chief Evans isn't going to do anything without the go-ahead from Marquette."

The five-minute drive to the center of town took two minutes and she and Kieran took the stairs two at a time. Kieran banged on Elena's locked office door.

"She's not here, Kieran."

"Then we hit the beaches. She said she wouldn't take him to a swimming beach. Where would she go?"

"Hold on." Devon crept down the hallway to Sam's office. She tried the handle, but he'd locked up for the day, too. Had he followed them to San Francisco thinking they had Michael with them? Or did he already know Michael was right here with Elena, the woman he'd charmed to get close to her son?

She shivered and hugged herself.

Kieran curled his arm around her shoulder. "Let's go. Give it your best guess. Where would Elena take Michael?"

"The beach at Columbella. You can't swim there. It has plenty of tidepools. The cave...and it's pretty deserted."

"What are we waiting for?"

They hopped back in the car and drove through town toward the beach at Columbella House.

"Look." Devon pointed to Elena's sedan parked in the turnout. "It's Elena's car."

Devon wheeled her car into the lookout area, her wheels crunching the gravel. They exited the car without taking in the view since an observer from this point couldn't see the beach below the house. That's why nobody but the locals came here. And if the locals planned to boogie board, surf or swim, they wouldn't come to Columbella Beach, which offered none of those activities.

They headed down the path on the side of the house and edged onto the rocks—the place where Devon had first laid eyes on her dead fiancé.

Cupping her hand over her eyes, she surveyed the narrow beach where the sun streaked through the encroaching fog. "They're not here."

"Maybe they went into the cave like you and Michael did that day."

Devon's cell phone rang and she tripped to a stop. "Hold on, Kieran. It's my phone."

Before answering, she glanced at the display and said to Kieran, "It's Detective Marquette."

"Put it on speaker and let's keep moving."

"Hello?"

"Ms. Reese, it's Detective Marquette. I did some investigating after you left."

She ignored his words and blurted out, "We think Michael witnessed the murder."

"What?"

"It was the dumbwaiter. It raised Kieran's suspicions when he saw it. He thinks Michael was in the dumbwaiter when Mrs. Del Vecchio was murdered."

"Are you with Michael now?"

"No." She licked her lips, salty from the ocean air and scanned the beach again. "He's supposed to be with his therapist, Elena Estrada, but she won't answer my calls and we don't know where they are."

Kieran nudged her forward, gripping her elbow as he pulled her back toward the path down to the beach.

"Listen to me carefully, Ms. Reese. I looked into Pelicano's background. He has a son—a son who's forty-five years old and who looks like his old man. Sammy Pelicano visited his father regularly and was with him at the end."

Devon tripped and crashed against Kieran's shoulder. "Sammy? Sam? Oh, dear God. It's him. It's him and he's with Elena and my son."

"I'm going to put in a call to the Coral Cove P.D.

We don't have any evidence against him. I'm putting him out there as a person of interest."

"Person of interest?" She gritted her teeth and picked her way along the path. "That's not going to get Chief Evans moving."

"I'm sorry. It's the best I can do right now. Michael's not even officially a missing person. We can't go in with guns blazing, Ms. Reese. It could compromise the case. We don't want to use illegal methods to bring this guy in and then have to let him out two hours after he gets his slick lawyer on the phone."

Kieran snatched the phone from her hand and hung up. "He can't go in with guns blazing, but I sure as hell can."

He charged ahead and Devon scrambled to keep up. Her breath came out in short spurts, more from fear than exertion.

"They're not here, Kieran. He must've taken them somewhere else. Maybe he met them here and sweet-talked Elena into going with him."

Kieran squinted his eye against the glare of the sun as it filtered through the haze. He turned his head from side to side, sweeping the empty beach. "Maybe they're in the cave."

"How could they be in the cave? The tide's coming in. If they had gone into the cave, they would've come out by now. Elena's a local. She knows how fast the tide can come in." Devon cupped her hands around her mouth. "Elena! Michael!"

Kieran pointed to the rocks stationed around the cave entrance, water sluicing over their smooth surfaces. "I'm going to check out the cave."

"I-if they're in the cave and not answering..." She clapped a hand over her mouth, preventing the rest of her horrible thought from finding words.

"It's a cave. Waves are crashing all around it. I don't think they'd hear you shouting."

"Okay. I'm coming with you."

Kieran stuck out his hand behind him and she grabbed on for dear life. It was a lot easier clambering over these rocks without water rushing over your feet.

She slipped and banged her knee, almost dragging Kieran down with her into the salty foam.

He turned, and hooking his arms beneath hers, hoisted her up. "Be careful and keep hold of my hand."

She had no intention of letting go. Her contact with Kieran's strong, capable hand was the only thing keeping her away from an abyss of panic and fear.

When he got to the cave entrance, Kieran poked his head inside and blocked Devon's way. He whispered, "I don't hear anything."

Devon stifled a sob. If Elena and Michael weren't on the beach where Elena had left her car, where had Sam taken them? They could be anywhere.

Kieran balanced a foot on a boulder. "I'm going inside. Something's not right."

Devon's heart galloped. She grabbed his back pocket. "I'm coming with you."

She scrambled onto the rock next to him and dropped to the sandy floor of the cave. "It's not flooded in here yet, but we don't have much time."

With one hand inching across the slippery, wet sea-cave wall, Devon crept into the cave, the fingers of her other hand tucked into Kieran's back pocket.

Her nostrils twitched at the briny smell and as the waves crashed on the outside walls, the noise created a rumbling in her chest.

Kieran stopped and her nose plowed into his back. "Devon, turn around and walk out."

His tight voice cut across the thundering waves and sliced into her gut. "What is it? What's wrong?"

"Go. Get out of here."

Bile rose from her belly, the sour taste flooding her mouth. Fear beat wings against her temples, and then adrenaline coursed through her system. If there was a choice between fight or flight, she'd learned to choose fight every time.

She shoved against Kieran's broad back. "I'm not going anywhere."

Kieran stepped aside, curling one arm around her waist and pulling her against him as if he feared she'd topple over if left on her own.

Her eyes adjusted to the gloom of the cave and her gaze dropped to the sandy floor.

A scream barreled up from her very depths as she stared into the lifeless eyes of Elena Estrada.

Chapter Fifteen

Devon choked and retched beside him. His hand cupped the back of her head and he pressed her face against his chest. He hadn't wanted her to see this. Elena had been Devon's friend. And she'd been Michael's guardian for the day.

He slammed his fist against the slimy cave wall. It was his fault. He'd encouraged Devon to leave Michael here when their son should've been with them. He didn't know the first thing about fatherhood.

Devon dropped to a rock near Elena's body. "Oh, my God. She's dead. She's dead. Where's Michael?"

She'd covered her face, but now her head jerked up. "Maybe he threw Michael off the rocks. Maybe he's already dead."

Kieran crouched beside her and gripped her arm. "Stop. Michael's not dead. We'll find him."

She turned wide, glassy eyes toward him. "We

need to find him. We need to call the police. Do you think Evans will listen to me now?"

"Of course." As Devon stood on shaky legs to retrieve her phone from her pocket, Kieran studied the crime scene. Pelicano had bashed Elena on the side of the head with a rock. One side of her head was sticky with blood. She may have seen it coming since one arm was outstretched, her fingers curled into a claw.

"Kieran, I can't find my phone. It must've fallen out of my pocket when I fell. Do you still have yours?"

"Mine ran out of juice yesterday. Yours might still be by that rock. There's not a lot of water yet."

He leaned forward to peer at the wet sand beneath Elena's fingers, not yet stiff with rigor mortis. She'd scratched at the sand.

Devon sobbed behind him. "I can't find my phone. We're wasting time."

He held up his hand. "Hold on. There's something here."

She leaned over his shoulder, her breathing erratic and raspy. "It's sand, wet sand."

"No, look." With one knuckle, he nudged aside Elena's cold fingers. "It's writing, Devon. She wrote something before she died."

Devon gasped and plunked onto the sand next to him. "What is it?"

He traced over the letters with his fingertip.

"The letters *C* and an *H. C, H.* Ch—something. That's not even Sam's name."

Devon gripped his arm, her fingernails biting into his flesh. "*C, H.* Columbella House. He took Michael to Columbella House."

Kieran pushed up to his feet taking Devon with him. "Why would Sammy Pelicano take Michael to Columbella House?"

"I don't know, but if Elena carved those letters into the sand with her dying breath, then they mean something." She slipped from his grasp. "We need to check Elena's pockets for a phone."

Kieran dipped back down and patted Elena's pockets and then turned her over to check the other pockets. "Empty. Don't worry about the phone right now. We need to get up to Columbella."

As they climbed over the first set of rocks, the water rushed in, soaking their shoes. Kieran scooped up Devon and lifted her onto the next boulder. "If we'd entered this cave ten minutes later, the water would've washed away Elena's message. Luck is on our side."

When they got clear of the cave, Devon tugged on his arm. "We can't go charging through the front door of the house if he's in there with Michael."

"What do you suggest?"

"You don't remember, do you? You don't remember the secret passage up from the beach through the basement of the house."

"If I don't remember, I'm glad you do. Lead the way."

Devon crossed the beach path to the other side of the cave and the rocks. The old house loomed above them, seemingly unreachable.

"The house is built into the rock. The first St. Regis had the builders tunnel down into the side of the cliff."

Devon led him into a shallow indentation in the side of the cliff. From the outside, it looked like another sea cave farther up the beach, but as they slipped into the entrance, a door appeared at the end of the passageway.

"Is it locked?"

"It's broken, like most everything at Columbella."

The sea air had rotted the solid wood door, but it still looked impenetrable.

Devon grasped the metal handle and yanked upward. "I can't do this by myself. You need to lift the door while I turn the handle."

Kieran crouched down and slid his hands in the space beneath the door. On the count of three, he heaved the door up and heard a click. He staggered backward as the door swung outward.

"Be careful. There are steps up to the basement."

He wedged the door shut behind them, and squeezed past Devon to the first step. "You stay behind me. I'm the one with the gun."

Their wet shoes squelching on the cement steps, they ascended to the bowels of Columbella House.

When he'd stayed here while watching Devon and Michael, he'd never ventured into the basement. He'd poked his head in the door once, but that had been enough. Dank and cold, the basement had given off a malevolent vibe.

It was no different now.

They reached the level floor, and Kieran helped Devon up the last few steps. Without a flashlight, the darkness closed in on them. They edged their way across the floor, littered with memorabilia from a few generations of long-ago St. Regises.

Devon's hand found his and she squeezed it. "Please tell me we're not too late for Michael."

"I just found my son. We can't be too late." He said the words to comfort Devon, but he believed them with his whole being. Fate had led him here to Coral Cove, to this house for this moment.

The dank moisture of the basement walls seeped into his flesh, chilling his bones. The remnants of past lives usually emitted an air of quaint comfort, but this memorabilia exuded hostility or at least an air of mystery and impenetrability.

He shook it off. He didn't come here to analyze the St. Regis history. He'd come here to rescue his son. And if he knew anything, it was how to bring down an enemy.

They picked their way through the debris to the basement stairs that led to the house. As they crept upward, Kieran said, "I already know that door is unlocked—broken. Now I just hope it doesn't creak."

He pushed it open with Devon hovering behind him, her breath hot on his back. The hinges protested, but only mildly.

Kieran stuck his head into the hallway that divided the kitchen from the curving staircase. He put a finger to his lips and closed his eyes, blocking out the sounds of his own breathing and his thundering heart, blocking out Devon's labored breathing behind him.

He listened to the house.

And then he heard it. Voices. Low, conspiratorial, hushed, harsh.

He tilted his head back, his nose in the air like a bloodhound on the scent. His nostrils flared. His muscles coiled. Every one of his senses clicked into high alert.

He pulled his weapon from his waistband and prowled forward on the balls of his feet.

He moved silently toward the voices coming from the library—that scorched testament to another man's lunacy. He held his arm out behind him to keep Devon back, but she knocked it away.

They both crouched outside the open door to the library, and Kieran pressed the side of his face against the wall. They must be inside the burned-out secret room. The voices continued, now within hearing range.

"Are you sure the doctor broad was telling you the truth?" A gruff voice, roughened by cigarettes and by hard time...and not Sammy Pelicano's.

Pelicano answered, "You told me yourself, the old lady said something about giving it to the kid and Elena verified that. I think he has it. I warned you not to hurt him, but you had to pull that stunt with the bathroom."

"What can I say? He saw me off Johnny Del's old lady, and then escaped up that shaft in the wall."

"The kid obviously hadn't told anyone what he saw. He never even told his therapist, although he did tell her about the money. And we need him alive to find that money."

"Well, wake him up then. The sooner we're out of here, the better. His hot mama along with that dangerous-looking dude with the eye patch will be coming back from the city any time now."

"No reason to think they'll come looking here. Especially since you shot at her the other night."

"I already told you, Sammy. I didn't shoot at her. I'm not dumb enough to leave any bullets that can be traced."

"No, just dumb enough to throw a Molotov cocktail through the window of a public bathroom."

The older man grumbled. "Wake up the kid already."

Kieran allowed one drop of relief to settle in his belly, but he didn't allow it to ease the tension that had seized his body, the tension he'd need to take out two enemies.

He couldn't see Michael from his position against the wall, couldn't see Pelicano and Mrs. Del Vecchio's killer.

But he didn't need to see.

"Wake up, kid."

Kieran's blood boiled when he heard the slap, and Devon stiffened beside him. He'd been so focused on the action in the hidden room, he'd almost forgotten Devon holding up the wall beside him. He wanted her far away from here, but wrenching her away from Michael would be an impossible task.

"Wake up."

Michael murmured and cried out.

Devon shifted beside Kieran, and he put a steadying hand on her twitching shoulder.

"Where's the bag with the money, kid?"

Sammy's partner cleared his throat and coughed. "We know the old lady gave it to you."

Michael started sniffling and rage poured

through Kieran's system. His finger tightened on the trigger of his weapon. His other hand curled into a fist.

Michael's high, clear voice rang out. "It's outside."

Devon sagged against the wall, and Kieran's lips tightened into a grimace. Was Michael telling the truth? Did he ever have any money?

He slipped a sidelong glance at Devon, who had one hand clamped over her mouth. Could it be true? Devon would've told him.

The older man snorted. "Outside? We're supposed to believe that?"

Michael's voice, steadier now, continued. "Outside with the shells. I left it there 'cuz I didn't want it anymore. Granny Del put it in my Thomas backpack."

Kieran's mind clicked back to his rescue of Michael from the rocks—a small figure weighed down by a colorful backpack, a backpack he claimed he'd lost.

He licked his lips. Could Michael convince these two to walk out of this room? Their greed should be enough of an incentive.

"What shells? What are you talking about? It's on the beach?"

"On the wooden thing outside with chairs. My daddy sat in those chairs."

The balcony. Had Michael left his backpack

on the balcony that first day Kieran had revealed himself? A backpack full of money?

"His daddy?" Johnny Del's old partner growled. "I thought he didn't have a daddy."

"It's the guy with the patch, who's probably on his way back from the city while we're standing here wasting time. Take us there, kid, and we'll let you go and won't bother your mommy anymore."

Kieran clenched his jaw. They had no intention of letting Michael go. Just like his captors hadn't had any intention of letting him go. Sometimes a man had to take extreme measures.

The shuffling in the room sent Kieran behind one of the dust covers, where he pulled Devon in beside him. He crouched on his haunches, peering through a slit in the white cover, every muscle in his body coiled.

Sammy came through the door first, a gun dangling from his hand, shoving Michael in front of him. An older man followed, his face craggy with the lines of a misspent youth.

Kieran touched Devon on the shoulder and mouthed, "Michael."

She nodded, and he knew he could count on her to keep their son out of danger. She'd done a helluva job for the first four years of Michael's life…with no help from him.

As the group passed in front of the table, Kieran

lunged for Sammy's legs. He hit him in the knees with a crack, ripping him from Michael's side.

Devon shot out like a flash and yanked Michael toward the desk covered with the white sheet.

Sammy screamed. "Go after the kid." Then he raised his gun and Kieran smacked his arm toward the ceiling. A shot rang out and plaster rained down on them.

The older man moved in on the desk where Devon was clawing at the dust cover and trying to reach for Michael at the same time. Kieran used his body to block them from the man's approach and then reached back and shoved Michael into Devon's arms. "Grab him."

As the older man barreled forward, fists first, a shot rang out.

Something skimmed Kieran's arm, but he took no notice. Fury pumped through his system, but he'd learned to focus after four years in captivity.

He swept his arm upward, cracking Sammy's elbow, driving the barrel of the gun toward the ceiling again. At the same time, Kieran swung his body around and landed a kick to the older man's midsection. The man doubled over and staggered back.

Sammy squeezed a third shot off at the ceiling and then leveled the gun at Kieran. Grabbing his wrist, Kieran shoved Sammy against the table with Devon and Michael crouched beneath.

The gun felt hot between their bodies, and Sammy still had his finger curled around the trigger. Kieran's nails bit into Sammy's forearm until his grip slackened and a life-and-death struggle ensued over the direction of the weapon.

Devon yelled, "Look out, Kieran!"

The older man lunged at Kieran's back, slicing his shoulder with a blade. Kieran drove his other shoulder into Sammy's chest and the gun blasted between them.

Sammy's blood soaked Kieran's shirt. He spun around and ducked another plunge of the knife grasped in the old man's hands. He grabbed one of his arms and twisted it behind him. Then in one quick movement, he stepped behind him and wrapped an arm around his throat. The man clawed at his arm with one hand, choking. Then he raised the hand with the knife and gripped the blade between two fingers. He drew his arm back, ready to launch the blade at Devon and Michael crouched beneath the table, fear coming off them in waves.

He was brutal. He was an animal. He had to save his family.

With one sharp twist, Kieran broke the neck of the man threatening his family.

The sea breeze played with the ends of Kieran's dark hair, shoved behind his ears. He'd removed his bloody shirt. His shoulder and upper arm sported fresh, white bandages, courtesy of the EMTs.

One ambulance and one coroner's van waited to take away the two dead bodies in Columbella House, and another ambulance was awaiting Elena's body from the cave.

Chief Evans scratched his chin. "So your son's the one who witnessed the murder?"

Devon glanced at Michael and shook her head at the chief. Was the man a complete idiot?

"Yeah, I saw that old man kill Granny Del." Michael kicked his toe against the crumbling step of the porch.

"I wish you would've told me, sweet pea." Devon brushed a finger along Michael's smooth cheek.

He hunched his shoulders. "I was scared."

"It's all over now."

"Is Dr. Elena coming back?"

Kieran gave a quick shake of his head, but Devon didn't need his advice on this one. "Dr. Elena is sad that her friend wasn't really a friend, so she went on a vacation."

Apparently, Michael hadn't witnessed Elena's murder in the cave. He didn't need to deal with the death of another person in his life right now.

"Sure you don't need to go to the hospital?"

The EMT put the finishing touches on Kieran's bandage.

"Nope, but I want you to check out my son. They shot him up with something to knock him out."

"It was a big needle, Daddy, but I didn't cry." Michael held out his two index fingers about six inches apart.

"You're one tough hombre." Kieran picked up Michael and deposited him on the edge of the ambulance. "But it's okay to cry. It's okay to admit you're scared."

The EMT shined a flashlight in Michael's eyes, and Kieran stepped away from the ambulance, pulling Devon with him.

"Chief Evans, did you say Detective Marquette was on his way?"

"Yeah. When he called to let us know the true identity of Sam, he told me he was taking a helicopter. That was over two hours ago, so he should be here anytime now. After you called me, I gave him an update."

Devon folded her arms. "If you had taken me seriously to begin with, maybe my son could've been spared further trauma."

"I don't think so, Devon. By the time you got here, Sammy Pelicano had already drugged your little boy and dragged Dr. Estrada into that sea cave."

Devon glanced at Kieran. "So who was that other man, the one who murdered Mrs. Del Vecchio?"

"Not sure yet." The chief lifted a shoulder. "But Marquette dug up some evidence that Sammy Pelicano was keeping company with one of Johnny Del's old cellmates."

"We figured something like that." Kieran winced as he rolled his shoulder. "You know, the old guy kept insisting to Pelicano that he didn't take a shot at Devon in Columbella House."

Evans snorted. "Why would he admit it? Men like that are so accustomed to lying, it's like second nature."

Devon wrinkled her brow. "He had a point in there, Kieran. Why shoot me if it was Michael they wanted?"

"Tell me something." The chief chewed on the toothpick shoved into the corner of his mouth. "Why did Pelicano keep Michael alive? If their plan was to get rid of the witness, why didn't they?"

Devon gasped and grabbed Kieran's arm. "The money. Do you believe he ever had the money?"

"What money?" Evans's gaze darted between her and Kieran.

"He must have. He told Elena about it, didn't he?"

"Looks like I missed all the excitement." Detective Marquette strode toward them, his shirt-sleeves rolled up and sweat dotting his brow.

"You're just in time." Devon jumped from the porch and walked toward the side of the house. "We think Granny Del may have given some of her husband's stash to Michael."

"What?" He and Chief Evans spoke in unison.

Devon continued her march to the side of Columbella House and the balcony over the sea. "That's why they kept Michael alive, thank God. They wanted him to take them to the money, to make sure he had it."

"Where would a kid keep hundreds of thousands of dollars?"

"In a Thomas the Tank Engine backpack, where else?"

The four of them made their way onto the balcony where Devon had spent her first moments with Kieran. Where Michael had left his prized backpack.

Her heart skipped two beats when she spotted the colorful pack in the corner of the balcony next to the basket of shells he'd examined on that day an eternity ago. It certainly didn't look like it could contain hundreds of thousands of dollars.

She pounced on the pack and unzipped it with unsteady hands. She peered inside and fell back on her heels. "Oh, my God."

The three men crowded in beside her and

Kieran reached into the pack. He drew out his hand and opened it. The small diamonds in his palm glittered and danced with fire in the setting sun.

"Why? Why would Granny Del give him these diamonds?"

"'Cuz she liked me." The EMT released Michael's hand and he skipped across the wooden slats of the deck. "She always gave me stuff."

Devon pulled Michael into her arms and squeezed him so hard he squirmed. "How did I not know this was going on?"

Kieran dropped the diamonds back in the bag and dangled it in front of Detective Marquette, who snatched it out of his hands. He and Chief Evans, heads together, made their way back to the front of the house.

Kieran dropped to the deck and sat cross-legged beside her and Michael, wrapping his arms around both of them. "How were you supposed to know about a couple of handfuls of diamonds?"

"When did she give them to you, Michael?"

He hunched his shoulders and his lower lip quivered. "She was nice."

"I know Granny Del was nice to you, but she had some bad friends." She kissed the top of his head. "Were you afraid to tell me because you were in the dumbwaiter where you weren't supposed to be?"

He nodded, and she bit her lip. Her fear caused words of anger to flood her mouth, but she swallowed them. He didn't need a scolding right now.... Maybe later, and maybe from his father this time.

"Did you like that hospital food?" She smoothed the tip of her finger along the curve of his ear.

Michael's eyes widened. "Yeah. I liked the pudding."

"Good, because we're sending you back there just to be on the safe side."

"And Daddy, too?" Michael tapped his finger against Kieran's bandages.

Kieran stretched up to his full height and scooped up Michael from the wooden deck. "Sure, I'll be there with you."

"What happened to the bad guys?"

"The bad guys are gone, Michael. They won't be around to scare you anymore."

Michael curled one arm around Kieran's neck. "You made them go away."

"Yep."

Devon scrambled to her feet and skimmed her hand along Kieran's shoulders. "Daddy will always be there to protect you, Michael."

Kieran leaned over and kissed her cheek. "I'll always be there to protect both of you.... If you'll have me, scars and all."

She returned the kiss to his chin. "I'll take you just the way you are."

And as she gazed into his dark eye, she still saw a hard man, a damaged man, a man with a quick temper and a steel edge...but still the man of her dreams.

* * * * *

Look for more stories in Carol Ericson's GUARDIANS OF CORAL COVE *miniseries later in 2012, wherever Harlequin Intrigue books are sold!*

LARGER-PRINT BOOKS!
GET 2 FREE LARGER-PRINT NOVELS PLUS
2 FREE GIFTS!

Harlequin®

INTRIGUE®

BREATHTAKING ROMANTIC SUSPENSE

YES! Please send me 2 FREE LARGER-PRINT Harlequin Intrigue® novels and my 2 FREE gifts (gifts are worth about $10). After receiving them, if I don't wish to receive any more books, I can return the shipping statement marked "cancel." If I don't cancel, I will receive 6 brand-new novels every month and be billed just $5.24 per book in the U.S. or $5.99 per book in Canada. That's a saving of at least 13% off the cover price! It's quite a bargain! Shipping and handling is just 50¢ per book in the U.S. and 75¢ per book in Canada.* I understand that accepting the 2 free books and gifts places me under no obligation to buy anything. I can always return a shipment and cancel at any time. Even if I never buy another book, the two free books and gifts are mine to keep forever.

199/399 HDN FERE

Name _____ (PLEASE PRINT) _____

Address _____ Apt. # _____

City _____ State/Prov. _____ Zip/Postal Code _____

Signature (if under 18, a parent or guardian must sign)

Mail to the **Reader Service:**
IN U.S.A.: P.O. Box 1867, Buffalo, NY 14240-1867
IN CANADA: P.O. Box 609, Fort Erie, Ontario L2A 5X3

Not valid for current subscribers to Harlequin Intrigue Larger-Print books.

**Are you a subscriber to Harlequin Intrigue books
and want to receive the larger-print edition?
Call 1-800-873-8635 today or visit www.ReaderService.com.**

* Terms and prices subject to change without notice. Prices do not include applicable taxes. Sales tax applicable in N.Y. Canadian residents will be charged applicable taxes. Offer not valid in Quebec. This offer is limited to one order per household. All orders subject to credit approval. Credit or debit balances in a customer's account(s) may be offset by any other outstanding balance owed by or to the customer. Please allow 4 to 6 weeks for delivery. Offer available while quantities last.

Your Privacy—The Reader Service is committed to protecting your privacy. Our Privacy Policy is available online at www.ReaderService.com or upon request from the Reader Service.

We make a portion of our mailing list available to reputable third parties that offer products we believe may interest you. If you prefer that we not exchange your name with third parties, or if you wish to clarify or modify your communication preferences, please visit us at www.ReaderService.com/consumerchoice or write to us at Reader Service Preference Service, P.O. Box 9062, Buffalo, NY 14269. Include your complete name and address.

HILP11B

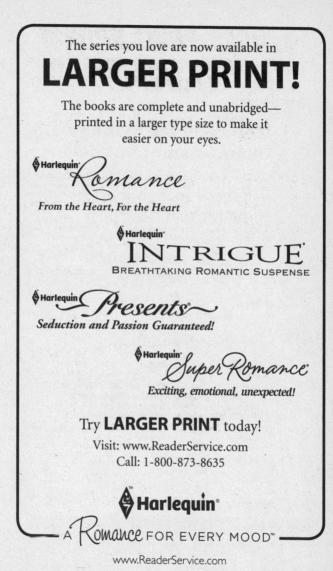